T HE

U NSPEAKABLE

Charles Laird Calia

T HE

U NSPEAKABLE

A NOVEL

William Morrow and Company, Inc. New York

It is the policy of William Morrow and Company, Inc., and its imprints and affiliates, recognizing the importance of preserving what has been written, to print the books we publish on acid-free paper, and we exert our best efforts to that end.

Library of Congress Cataloging-in-Publication Data

Calia, Charles Laird.
The unspeakable : a novel / by Charles Laird Calia.
    p.   cm.
ISBN 0-688-15119-1
I. Title
PS3553.A39867U5 1998
813'.54—dc21
97-36049
CIP

Printed in the United States of America

First Edition

1 2 3 4 5 6 7 8 9 10

BOOK DESIGN BY LEAH S. CARLSON

www.williammorrow.com

For Brenda,
Cameron,
and Cassie

NOUS CORRIGEONS LE VICE DU
MOYEN PAR LA PURETÉ DE LA FIN.

*We correct the fault of our methods
by the purity of our ends.*
—PASCAL

THE

UNSPEAKABLE

Not Lourdes but a church in Minnesota.

Kneeling, a young girl, ten or eleven years old, dressed in white linen, cups her hands in supplicant fashion. Her knees grope along the floorboards of the pew, slight pressure as the cushions give, spreading out, buckling upward. As do her eyes. Drawn to the face of our risen Lord, beardless, hair cropped short and smiling, nothing like the pictures from Sunday school. He looms above her, fingers in the air, the bread of life already broken.

"Do this in memory of me."

Crossing herself she offers up a prayer with her right hand, sign language, for the girl is deaf; then she gobbles up the remaining host from sight. Crumbs linger, a speck of eternity here and there, but they are quickly licked up by a mouth hungry for salvation.

The Lord again: "This cup that is poured out for you is the new covenant in my blood. Take and drink. And inherit eternal life."

Inherit eternal life.

The girl takes the chalice, her eyes fixed on the Lord, who carefully spells out each word, one by one. She fingers the cheap edge of the cup with its stamped pictures of dead saints and apostles, and raises it. A long swallow. The swallow from the desert, parched and dry. A thousand years dry.

The girl crosses herself again, stands, and not more than a few

❦

steps from the altar exclaims with a shrill but damaged voice the good news:

"I can hear!"

HOLY WEEK, 1991.

I'm sitting in the church where it all began. For several months now I have been receiving mysterious accounts, reports scribbled anonymously on the backs of old church programs, flyers, pages torn from hymnals, and then sent to me through the Archdiocese of St. Paul. Their author is unknown to me. But the reports are all similar. They show one person or another being healed, the lowly, the sick, the afflicted, not by physicians or hospitals but by one man. A priest.

The individual in question, Jim Marbury, possesses no special or mystical abilities that I'm aware of. He cannot read minds, nor can he levitate like some carnival magic act. He cannot raise himself from the dead, not even with the power of God, nor can he calm the storms on Lake Minnetonka or the Sea of Galilee. He knows this; at least, I believe he knows this despite suggestions to the contrary. Many in his congregation actually believe they have been healed of one malady or another by Marbury. Most of these healings have been minor, psychological at best, curing such things as colds and lumbago. But a few of them have defied all known science. At least they claim to.

These healings, always performed at night with a small prayer service, have few of the benefits that modern technology can provide. No cameras are there to record the events. No microphones, no skeptical doctors to perform examinations before and after, nothing but a shared experience. Even the reports that I've received have that fast, almost staccato writing, as though the author was swept in as well, believing what he or she knows is unbelievable. Not that knowing what to believe is always so easy. The real story is often difficult to track down. Documents fade. Witnesses forget or embellish. People up and vanish. My own attempts at finding firsthand the participants in these healings have largely been futile.. Part of this I blame on the nature of this congregation, a special voice- and hearing-impaired church located in South Minneapolis. Many of the members are poor, often castoffs from the mainstream church, and they seem to exist on the fringes of the rest of society. Apartments aren't always there. Phone numbers are faked or just don't exist. As for church records, they haven't been updated in years.

Some folks drift off as well. The healed deaf girl, for one, off to Montana or some such place, and the truth along with her. Forget about finding her at school or tracking down her parents. They're gone. None of this surprised Marbury, who knew the conditions here when he accepted the call, or rather begged for it once that he knew that it was available. Several priests have come and gone in the last two years alone, each one telling me exactly how difficult it was to minister. The church was often empty or sparsely attended, and those that did show up sat glassy-eyed and uninterested. Donations, always meager, sunk to new lows. Bills were left unpaid. Heat was turned down in the winter, doors left open in the summer to save on air conditioning. But worse, the gospel began to sound like reading the local newspaper, void of hope, a droning repetition for people that already knew enough of repetition.

And then Marbury arrived.

I began receiving these reports soon after. And not just stories about healings but other stories as well. Stories about people working together, holding baking contests to raise money, and joining painting crews for much needed repairs. Stories too of people praying together, and building something here that before never existed. A real community.

Marbury scoffed when I asked him if he was responsible, not just for the healings, but for it all.

"I'm just a pipeline," he said, "not the fuel. God's that."

He spoke in sign language. The language of his church.

"What about the deaf girl?"

"Folks get better. What can I say, Peter?"

And that's how it began.

But this wasn't the real beginning. That started in Iowa when we first met almost twenty years ago. It was at seminary, and Marbury was thrust into my life in the most conspicuous of ways. We were neighbors, living on the same floor. But even back then he was evoking the name of God to wiggle out of his jams, theological or otherwise, spinning us all into mental circles. God, claimed Marbury, quoting the prophet Isaiah, controlled all aspects of life. Light and darkness, weal and woe. As I imagine He controls the whimsy of healing. Prayers are offered, even the laying on of priestly hands. And despite the fact that the hands are human, the voice now silenced, the prayers recited in sign language, people are, remarkably, healed. They are healed, it is said, as a testament to faith. Not in the spiritual world above us, nor even around us, but rather, faith that Jim Marbury, a man who in his youth had the voice of a cool radio disc jockey, lost it so he could hear the word of God more clearly.

For Marbury himself was mute.

Almost five months have passed since he returned from the trip that changed his life and altered his voice and faith irreparably. For better or worse, the doctors who studied Marbury after his ordeal, including the top neurologists and surgeons around, were all stumped. Prior examinations have concluded nothing was abnormal, and even state-of-the-art procedures like CAT scans and MRIs uncovered no physical reasons for his affliction. That Marbury doesn't speak is a given. But not, according to medical opinion, because he can't. His vocal cords and larynx, which pieces everything together, are completely normal, except when Marbury opens his mouth nothing comes out.

The church then, in her infinite wisdom, has concluded that Marbury doesn't wish to speak. Psychiatrists support this claim only by noting the evidence, that Marbury should be able to say something. That he doesn't seems a matter of volition, whether his own or God's, nobody can say. One idea floated about is that Marbury doesn't speak for political reasons. By portraying himself as a mute priest in an even more silent church he hammers home some metaphor about his congregation, highlighting I suppose the social and economic plight of his flock. An interesting idea and one that I myself might subscribe to if not for one thing. Marbury knows why he is silent and he'll mention it anytime he is asked. God took his voice, he says, presumably because the Almighty needed it more. A nutty idea, made only nuttier by the fact that his congregation seems to agree with him. It was a point that made everyone at my office, my supervisor included, quite nervous.

"Something's brewing, Whitmore. I can smell it. And it stinks."

The voice was Bishop Anton T. Fellows, D.D., of the Archdiocese of St. Paul, a squat man with an almost supernatural hankering for Cuban cigars who shifted his weight back and forth in his chair like a brass pendulum. We sat and reviewed the documents about Marbury and the healings in his office, but the more the Bishop read, the more disturbed he became.

Finally he said, "You know how that business in Portugal got started. A few kids seeing visions. And now look. Gads, a goddamn spectacle."

Smoke, acrid and dense, clouded his own vision.

"What's next? A gift shop, postcards? You're his friend, you tell me."

My voice: "A long time ago, maybe."

"Well, I don't want to hear about his face appearing in the clouds or on the cover of the *National Enquirer,* do you understand me?"

I understood too clearly.

My real job, if anyone actually asked me, would probably sound like something closer to that of a character out of a Mickey Spillane novel than that of a priest. My official role and title, as a Vicar for the Diocese, assigned I might add by the Bishop for this specific case, requires a variety of skills, not all of them advertised in the job description. Like investigating an old friend. In short, I face problems both theological and practical with Marbury, and my job, at least here, is to uncover the exact details of his affliction, details that if widely known might put individuals or the church at large in an embarrassing, if not compromising, position. Throughout my tenure in this office, now almost fifteen years, I have seen everything the papers in other locales have reported and more. Embezzlement, sexual abuse, infidelities of every kind, committed by both laity and priests. Many of these cases, unknown to the general public, are unknown for a variety of reasons, negotiation and tact only being two, along with a healthy scorn for the press. Scorn that Marbury didn't always seem to share.

"Your work's cut out for you, Peter. He likes reporters."

The position, as one can imagine, carries with it a certain amount of implicit power, held though not always used, not terribly unlike that of an agent at Internal Revenue. Fear has much to do with that, or rather, the perception of something to fear. For the very fact that I'm investigating means that something is there worthy to investigate. In Marbury's particular case, it's the truth that I'm after. But more than that, a disavowal that he isn't what he's perceived to be by everyone around him. A man touched by God.

"I warned him," said the Bishop. "But he thinks this is a democracy."

I knew that it wasn't, evidenced by my assignment.

"He won't talk to me, despite my being his friend," I said.

The Bishop just smiled. "He'll talk to you. It's called trust."

• • •

Regardless of the fact of our past friendship, even one so long ago, I cannot claim to have kept in touch with Marbury. The years have separated us, each of us staying in his own little world. Mine was here, at the Diocese, while Marbury pursued other matters. First, a brief stint at a parish in New Ulm, Minnesota, where he received glowing reports for his activities, and then in Minneapolis, where he started and ran a shelter in one of the poorer neighborhoods. His success was something that I had heard about of course. I did follow his career with some scrutiny, especially his growing presence on television and in the print media, where he was popular as a social commentator, but our paths had yet to cross.

Not that I didn't think about him. In a sense, he never left my mind. A word or odd quote would pop up unexpectedly, buried in those long years between youth and middle age, and I would think about him. Perhaps it was something that he never said, just imagined by me to fill in a popular view or a view that I wished I really had, I don't know. At any rate, Marbury was in my mind engaging and captive, a man who if he had never existed would be someone I would create a thousand times over.

But for all the wrong reasons.

When I told Marbury this, my thoughts about him over the years, he just smiled. His long body stretched out in the pew, taking it over. Marbury's church, the church where we were sitting, was a simple one. The seats were made of a rough-hewn wood, hardly varnished. Behind the altar, a black cloth hung from a cross made of bolted-together two-by-fours in anticipation of Good Friday, only a few days away. We sat there and talked.

"I was an asshole back then," he said. "Didn't you think?"

My own knowledge of sign language, self-taught, I'm afraid, and somewhat rusty, I learned on behalf of the deafness in my own family, namely that of my sister, Sandra. I was the only one in the family who knew it, and as children we spoke often. Now I was using it again with Marbury, except that instead of replying in sign, I spoke. Words, as if to defy the silence, and to remind him that the church was watching. That I was watching.

"Oh, come now, you can speak. Be glad for that."

I was diplomatic. "You seemed to be in your own world in seminary."

"That's because I didn't want to be in yours."

I looked at Marbury. Studied him more like it. His body was lean, a thin ribbon of muscle and sinew held together by God knows what. His face was thinner than I remembered it, more drawn, though the eyes still had that translucent quality to them. Blue, like the marbles children used to play with. His hair was shorter than it was in seminary. Hardly the chest and chains look before I knew him, before he joined the seminary, though I saw the pictures. A regular hippie, Marbury trimmed the hair and beard to make himself look as if he belonged, though I sometimes questioned whether he ever really did.

I thought about what he said and asked, "Then why did you become a priest in the first place? If you didn't want this world, why be here at all?"

He smiled. "Do you really want to know?"

"Yes."

"Then curse *Playboy* magazine. I was paging through, getting my fill of the various models, when I found an ad. Only a Jesuit would write an ad."

"What kind of an ad?"

"For the priesthood. It was famous, I'm shocked you haven't seen it."

I leaned back, somewhat amused. The ad that Marbury was referring to I had only heard about, not seen, but I knew that it was real. It was somebody's idea of a desperate appeal for more priests, I think, at a time when ordination in the priesthood was down drastically. As good a shot as any, I suppose, though I didn't think people actually responded to this sort of a thing, something I told Marbury.

This remark must have struck him as humorous, for he laughed. No sounds of course, except for that little croaking, breathing more like it, but I took it as laughter anyway.

"Imagine my shock as well," he said, his hands almost moving faster than my ability to translate, "looking at a centerfold only to be upstaged by God. Well, not God, not that time at least, but envoys. If you want to call Iowa an envoy."

"You're telling me that you responded to an advertisement?"

Marbury just smiled. It was his inspiration, the ad. Later he found the addresses of several seminaries and, in typical fashion, just closed his eyes and picked one out by chance. Or rather, God picked one out for him.

He picked Iowa.

Marbury said, "I drove there myself. Someone suggested the Greyhound, God's wheels, cheap, a confession in every seat, but I wanted a way out. Just in case."

When I started seminary in the fall of 1971, Marbury, already a year ahead of me and years wiser, still had that car. It was an old Volvo with a shredded blue interior. Ten years old at least, the car rattled and clanked when it started, knocking off pieces of the dashboard while warming up. A cab light stayed on all the time as I recall, a weird kind of metaphor that illuminated a backseat that was always packed and ready to go, loaded up with duffels and half-opened boxes, in case the urge struck Marbury to flee. But it never did.

Not that any one of us was firm on staying. We were a small seminary, a hundred students at best, floating in like human balloons from the Vietnam War. Some hiding, others just escaping for a short time. We lived in a series of poorly maintained buildings on a bluff overlooking the Iowa River, near Decorah, in a pastoral community with farms and woodlands. Our seminary was one of the few industries in town, and except for a rival bunch of Lutherans, the only seat of higher learning in these parts. I arrived, as did many of my peers, excited but somewhat nervous about my future and the challenges that lay ahead. Nervous too about my convictions, which I deemed shaky at best. Naturally I had grown up Catholic, or mostly so, my father embracing the faith of my mother as he got older, and if not for the pressures from both family and country, I might never have chosen such a life for myself. Tradition, they called it. My mother at least called it that—tradition—though I had another name for it.

My mother's side of the family, as I was constantly reminded, had always done their part through the years for God and Nation, supplying both with eager recruits. Recruits for war, recruits for the ministry. As fate would have it, I was born in the midst of change. Vatican II had taken its toll among the growing counterculture that made joining the priesthood, except for reasons to evade the draft or just wanting to be around other men, nearly unthinkable. But my mother, ever the optimist when it came to issues of the faith, especially faith in the holy machinery, summed things up quite differently.

She said, "What an exciting time, Peter. It's a new church, with new opportunities. Who knows where you could go. Bishop, maybe. Dare I even say it? Right to the Holy See."

I, of course, saw my chances in Rome as remote at best, but my mother had a point. The ministry was calling and it was my duty, indeed my ancestral destiny, to respond. My uncle was a priest, along with some other relatives, each one charting his way through the past like some familial apostolic succession. We Whitmores could trace part of our Catholic lineage back to popes long since dead, and our service was well documented. Monks, teachers, parish administrators, anywhere the calling led us. My mother reminded me of these servants as I boarded the Greyhound for Iowa, ironically the same bus from Minneapolis that Marbury had scoffed at. She kissed me good-bye, her lips touching my cheeks in the softest manner, as I imagine mothers sending their children off to die. "Carry with you the pride of the family," she said. I remember those words as the doors swished shut, heavy diesel in the air, a black cloud blocking out everything, my pride included.

Marbury was there waiting for me as I left the bus. We didn't speak except for a hello, but then we didn't have to. His mere presence spoke volumes. In one moment, Marbury had cut down every image I had ever had of the priesthood. Maybe it was the jeans and sandals that he wore, though others had adopted that same way of dressing. Or maybe it was just the way that he carried himself, aloof yet with a watchful eye. He was always alert, on the lookout it seemed. Later I heard stories about him. Other students, apparently feeling sorry for me having Marbury living next door, filled me in on the gossip. Rumors circulated about Marbury dodging the draft, dodging the police as well, with wild stories ranging from theft to drugs. For his part, always coy, Marbury confirmed or denied nothing. And this only made people talk more. Our superiors gave more fuel to the rumors when I heard one of them tell another, "Christ took sinners into the fold. Who are we not to do the same?" And from that moment on I saw Marbury as our very own Mary Magdalene, who traded one life for the best one offered.

When I told Marbury about my first impressions of him, especially just walking off the bus, he smiled.

He said, "I was a loose torpedo back then. Still am."

I nodded. It was something that I couldn't disagree with.

"But then you're here, aren't you? You know that already."

"Talk spreads. It isn't every day that people feel the presence of God."

"Oh, that—"

He waved me off with his nonspeaking hand as if a response wasn't even worthy. But then he reconsidered, saying, "That's just the voice, Peter. Or lack of one. People want to relate. Deep inside they want you to feel what they feel, you know that. Some go too far."

"And how far is that? Healing people?"

"I never said I could heal."

"You don't have to. People say it of you," I said.

"Do you believe everything people say?"

"When it's about a priest, I listen."

"Then what's the word on you, Peter?"

I looked at Marbury, studied him with a burning glance. "Just that I'm a good priest, I hope. What you should be."

"Oh, you're questioning my goodness now."

"Only your intentions, Marbury."

"My best intentions," he said, looking away, "I left in a snowstorm a thousand miles from here."

The snowstorm.

Marbury's trip to Pennsylvania, and the subsequent blizzard that followed, is generally agreed upon to be the dividing line between the old Marbury and this one. Before Philadelphia and the conference that lured him out there, Marbury was a priest like any other, exuding nothing so unusual or scandalous that would warrant the attention of this office. We were naturally aware of his talents, especially the uncanny knack he had for creating interest and furor over any project that he took on. This was particularly true of his shelter, which he started after an encounter with the homeless.

The story went like this:

One night, while walking home from a hospital visit, Marbury came across a man sleeping outside. The man was huddled inside a sleeping bag, freezing and hungry, but Marbury offered no help. He just walked on, like most people do, forgetting the incident altogether. That night the temperatures plunged well below zero

Manuel, assuming that Marbury was necessarily delayed or even had canceled without notice, failed to report his absence to conference authorities for another three days. Add to that the missing travel time and Marbury was unaccounted for almost a week, the time in question.

A few of these days I can vouch for myself. On Sunday, December 2, Marbury checks the weather and gases up his car at a local Fina, for which purchase I have a copy of the credit receipt. He drives I-94 east through Wisconsin and Illinois, and I have another receipt from a Super 8 motel, right outside of Elkhart, Indiana, where he spends the night. Monday, December 3, after a breakfast of cereal, danish, and coffee, Marbury prepares for the long day's journey across the rest of Indiana and Ohio, then into Pennsylvania. He is warned, at least according to a waitress that I interviewed by phone, who remembers Marbury because of his generous tip, of an impending storm, one centered around the Great Lakes, with all the moisture associated with these lake storms, and it was moving rapidly. But Marbury ignores this information and drives on anyway, hoping to beat out the weather.

Obviously a fateful decision.

Marbury heard my version of the events only to correct them with a quick sweep of his hands.

He said, "Breakfast was bacon and eggs. Nothing mystical there."

I nodded and opened up my notebook, where along with my file on Marbury I had assembled some of the various accounts from people who knew and worked with him, including the nurses and doctors who handled his case as he was recuperating, after the incident, here in Minneapolis. As far as I knew, no one had heard the entire story before, not even the authorities in Pennsylvania.

"You're writing this down?" he asked.

"I have to, you know that."

"Then you better get the facts right."

Marbury explained that he had most of the day's driving under his belt when it started. A light rain at first, outside of Cleveland. It didn't stop him, he said; if anything the rain just made him push harder. At least until he hit the Allegheny Mountains.

"Why didn't you stop in Pittsburgh," I asked, "instead of continuing?"

"I really thought it would end. Despite the forecast, there were peeks of sun."

The radio, admitted Marbury, contradicted all of this. Dire predictions of a blizzard filled every station. Warnings of ice storms, massive whiteout conditions, road drifts, and snows of near biblical proportions were predicted. But he didn't listen. Marbury swung past Pittsburgh and into the mountains, through one of those famous long tunnels, and when he emerged again, it started. Snow. Big flakes at first, like in one of those Christmas shake-ups, then gradually harder.

Shelter was being advised on the radio. And many of the roads, now covered and drifting, were becoming impassable. Marbury said that he would have kept on driving that night, probably to his own doom, if not for the one thing that stopped him.

The accident.

Ahead of him blue and red lights cut through the falling snow, obviously the police. In the distance Marbury said that he could see a car, all crushed up like an accordion and turned on its side. Several men in green parkas hovered about, with crowbars, working to free someone. Anyone. Marbury said that he slowed down to a crawl as he approached, out of respect partially, but also because he could no longer see. The snow was now moving in wild swirls, and the men with the crowbars almost had to brace themselves against the wreck to stay upright, or risk getting blown over and down a ravine by the wind.

Suddenly one of them waved and staggered forward. Marbury

stopped the car and waited for the green parka to catch up, then in one breath:

"We got a bad one here, mister. The snow's cut off anything behind you. Ahead, God knows. You might want to follow us back to town for the night."

Marbury agreed and let the engine idle. The scene looked bad. The car had spun into an embankment and then into a tree that almost cleaved it in two. A body was lying next to the car, bloody and unconscious, or maybe dead, Marbury couldn't tell. Someone was working frantically on the body, but the wind and snow just wouldn't cooperate, blowing pieces of the car, a torn airbag, and parts of the dashboard all around.

And then the man in the parka again:

"You're a priest, aren't you? If ever we needed one, Father."

I interrupted Marbury at this part of his story, an easy thing to do given that I still had a speaking voice and asked him, "How could he have possibly known that?"

"Clergy sticker. It came with the car."

"But it was snowing."

"I had to clean the windshield with my glove, it was that bad."

I nodded and wrote this down. I wrote down everything that Marbury told me for several reasons, not the least being that it was a way for me to organize and structure my own thoughts. Often an investigation would take me where the other person was comfortable going, and I had to be comfortable as well. Even if I didn't always believe in where I might end up.

Marbury went back to the story without missing a beat. He said that a body was lying on a stretcher now, clearly that of a woman, maybe middle-aged. Her body was limp, absolutely lifeless.

The man in the parka again:

"She stopped breathing once, Father. I can't say she'll make it."

Marbury reached into his glove compartment for a Bible. He

stepped out of the car, the snow and wind driving at his body, and made his way to the stretcher. His feet plunged into the snow and back out again, leaving only deep holes.

Another man screamed:

"I'm losing her!"

Marbury trudged faster. When he got to the woman he said that he fell on his knees, not out of prayer or sorrow, for he didn't know this woman, but because the wind had knocked him down.

"Father!"

On his knees, Marbury started to pray.

As I listened to this story, actually Marbury's retelling of it, I watched the way that he spoke, how forceful his hand actions were, the way he reenacted it perfectly. Every line seemed to weave in at the exact moment, neither detracting from the story nor inflating it unnecessarily. But there was something else. Marbury spoke so convincingly that I felt that I was really there, and the event was right before my eyes when I closed them. I could see everything. From the cops to the woman dying on the stretcher, and that perhaps was the very thing that fascinated me most.

The woman.

In my job, I know of few dying women. My duties as a priest are now strictly administrative, pushing papers and such, but I do miss the energy of a ministry like Marbury's. I bury no one, and except for my attendance at official functions, I might just as easily forget that death exists. Or rather, that I was trained to play a part in it.

"What do you say in these instances," I asked, "when you pray?"

Marbury gave me a strange look. "I pray for God's will."

He was doing just that when the sound of bending metal stopped him. The workers were digging in the wreck again, this time with blowtorches and blankets, which meant only one thing. Someone else was still in the car. Marbury said that he went back to his prayers but could concentrate only on the torch, which sounded like a wild snake hissing and thrashing about in the wet snow. He was about to give up on the prayers altogether, close his Bible and walk off, when he heard a loud voice. It was a child.

One of the workers:

"She's in here. Christ, I can't believe it!"

More commotion and bending metal. Several men in parkas rushed in with spare hands, and great pieces of the car began to shake and move. Then someone reached in and pulled out the victim, a young girl, hardly more than three or four. She looked cold, though otherwise healthy. A worker wrapped a blanket around her, mummy-style, and ran her over to a Ford Bronco, which was now serving as a makeshift ambulance. On the side of the vehicle, Marbury noticed a faded decal that through the falling snow read WHEELERSBURG POLICE.

The little girl, now alert, was given another blanket and a glass of water, which she quickly drank. Somebody looked her over and concluded that she was all right, remarkably uninjured. Her eyes darted around, checking out the men and vehicles until she saw the bloody woman on the stretcher, her body now being carried into the truck. The girl winced slightly, but didn't cry.

One of the men in the parkas said:

"Your mommy's hurt, but we'll do our best. OK?"

The little girl nodded slowly, again with no emotion.

"She's going to the hospital, where doctors can help her."

The man snapped his fingers. "Do you understand me?"

"Shock," said another voice. "Let's move."

The stretcher was pushed in next to the little girl, who was placed to make room in the truck. One of the men in the parkas, a paramedic, cupped a plastic respirator around the woman's mouth and turned it on. But she didn't breathe.

Someone looked at Marbury. "She needs God now, I'm afraid."

"Not in front of the girl," barked the paramedic.

"Oh, she's not all here anyway."

❦

But the man was wrong.

The little girl saw the woman, and like in some movie, reached over with her hand and touched her on the forehead. What happened next, said Marbury, was nothing short of confusion. The woman on the stretcher, one moment ago dead or steps away from death, suddenly opened her mouth and gasped for air. She gasped like a swimmer underwater who was surfacing quickly and from the depths, that much.

"Did you see that?" yelled the paramedic. "She moved!"

But somebody else had doubts. "Nerves. Those are just nerves."

"Sure, an involuntary reaction," said another.

And then the woman took another breath, louder than before.

"Is that involuntary, Father?" asked the paramedic. "You tell me."

Marbury leaned over the woman and heard her breathing. It was faint, but breathing nonetheless. He shook his head.

"That," he said carefully, "that I call a miracle."

"Miracles now. Face it, Whitmore. He's pulling our leg."

The Bishop stood at a large French window, his back away from me. I could see his fingers tapping nervously against his thigh, as though debating something, but he wouldn't tell me what. I had already informed him about my meeting with Marbury the previous day, and the story that he told me about the accident. But he didn't seem to care about hearing any more.

He just said, "Your advice. Remind me to ignore it next time."

My advice.

What the Bishop was referring to, what he always had tucked away in his back pocket for my humiliation, was this. It was my recommendation that gave Marbury his current position. After he was found in Pennsylvania, debate raged over what to do with him. A few on our staff suggested an extended leave, rest mostly, in hopes that he would regain his faculties and go back to work. Even the Bishop liked that idea. But I knew Marbury. I knew that if something was bothering him, even if he was on the verge of cracking up, losing his mind altogether, no amount of rest would help him out of it. He needed to work his way free. So I suggested an option, a new job, and pushed hard for it to happen.

The Bishop went along, reluctantly. He had serious reservations

❦

about Marbury identifying with this new congregation, a voice-
and hearing-impaired church that I had selected for him, and wondered, if not to himself, then aloud, whether Marbury would take
this as an official seal of approval for his actions. The call was a
difficult one, I knew that. And Marbury would throw every ounce
of energy into it, I hoped, eventually giving up this business about
his voice altogether just to survive.

He had to. The church was famed for its difficulty. Priests
came and went with frightening ease. One stayed on for only a
month before asking for a reassignment. Another left under
cloudy circumstances, citing emotional duress. Some of the blame,
I'm afraid, rests with this office. Many of these men were woefully
prepared for service in a congregation where only a handful of its
members spoke or could hear, and that pressure alone, the isola-
tion, drove several out. But Marbury wasn't as easy to drive away.
For one, he was already mute and isolated, so he seemed to fit
right in. And the news of serving there, devastating to some men,
liberated Marbury and sent his spirits soaring. That was three
months ago.

The healings began shortly thereafter. Marbury instigated a
prayer service for various petitions, including personal ailments. My
reports tell me that in the beginning the prayers were benign, as
well as the cures. But one day a woman appeared in a wheelchair,
depressed, almost lifeless. Marbury prayed over her and apparently
got carried away, for he called on the power of the Almighty to cure
this woman, to cure in fact everything about her. The woman,
thinking that God was listening or either just from plain spiritual
exuberance, stood up from her wheelchair and walked.

She kept right on walking.

Or so say my reports. Fortunately for me and this office, these
notes have fallen into no other hands but my own, thank God. The
newspapers clamor in these parts, as I'm sure they do everywhere,

for any kind of news. The more sensational, the better. And in a world of electronic mail and fax machines, bad news travels faster than in times past. Rumors of all kind are only a videotape away, and then a real mess. *Hard Copy* or supermarket tabloids. Although it could have been worse. Had Marbury been tucked away in some tiny congregation in Iron or Fifty Lakes, some place far-off, in the woods or on the prairie, the Diocese might never have noticed. But here, right beneath our noses, the Bishop had no other choice than to act. And act he must.

The Bishop tugged on the end of a cigar, pensively.

He said, "I could make a case for excommunication, you know."

But that wasn't the Marbury that I knew, a man who would want to toss away everything that he had worked so hard for, and I told the Bishop that.

He just shook his head. "Unless he's gone mad. He might be mad."

"He isn't mad, I assure you."

"Then what?"

I shrugged. "Maybe I can reason with him."

"Reason? He's personally absolving sins now, Whitmore. Only God does that."

"Where did you hear that from?"

"The church secretary."

"Surely, she's mistaken."

"He's healing people like God. Why not go all the way?"

I felt a brush of smoke crash against my body.

"Yes, yes . . . your wonderful advice," the Bishop said.

"I didn't know it would come to this."

"You and the Sanhedrin both."

Then his last words.

He said, "They tried to clean up their mess. Might I suggest you try to do the same."

. . .

I went back to Marbury's church later that afternoon, and walked in unannounced. But Marbury was nowhere to be found. Not in his office, not in the sanctuary, not even in the bathroom, where I looked. I began to feel like he had cut out on me, stood me up, and I was about to leave when a finger tapped me on the shoulder from behind. It was Marbury holding a tray of fresh coffee.

"Where were you?" I asked.

"Oh, I'm around."

He smiled weakly and handed me one of the Styrofoam cups. I could see that Marbury had already drunk some of his, a tidy row of little teeth marks around the edge of his cup. His trademark. Every cup in seminary, at least the plastic ones, seemed to carry that mark, like that of an animal. Marbury was always scenting out his territory for others to heed.

As he still was.

I followed him into the sanctuary and plunked myself down. Too closely perhaps, for he slowly wiggled away from me and my notes, which started an encroaching tide toward him. Marbury winced a few times at the amount of paper that was coming out of my briefcase, the signed affidavits and testimonials, along with a map of Pennsylvania, which I spread out in large sections over my knees.

Marbury smiled. "A man of many talents. Map keeper, investigator."

The word "investigator," despite the fact that Marbury was signing, just seemed to hang in the air and float between us. I had always viewed myself as a priest just like Marbury, not working in quite the same world perhaps, yet still contributing to the faith. But I knew he wasn't as certain.

"How is the good Bishop anyway?" he asked, out of the blue.

"He's troubled. You have us wringing our hands."

"What on earth for?"

"I think it's obvious. Prayer services. People hearing again."

"You're making me sound like God."

"Do you see yourself as God?"

Marbury just sipped his coffee. Stony silence.

I said, "I'm just thinking about the deaf girl. She must."

"The uniform, Peter. Representatives and all that."

"I've been told you absolve people of their sins now."

"From whom?"

"Does it matter?"

"Well, it's ridiculous."

I nodded and went back to my notes, trying to find out exactly where we had left off. But my concentration was broken by Marbury laughing, or rather convulsing in his seat.

"What is it?"

"Do you remember Price, the fellow with the pants?"

I thought for a moment and then it came back to me. Dwayne Price.

"From seminary?"

Marbury nodded like an anxious child.

Dwayne Price, the fellow in question, was a gangly man, built more like a cornstalk half wilted in the heat than anything else. He was also one of those fellows who seemed to enter our world by sheer coincidence, if not by mistake. For only a grave error could have placed Price in the seminary to begin with. He was a man with no social graces, who left the door of the toilet open while he did his business. But that wasn't even the worst of it. He enjoyed it. He especially enjoyed sitting there singing, his bright yellow pants, the one's Marbury was referring to, wrapped clear down around his ankles. Price would sit there for hours, doing nothing but singing.

"I never saw him off the toilet," I said.

"Only a few times. When he needed more paper."

"Maybe it was the food."

✤

"Maybe it was his head, Peter. A real cuckoo."

Marbury was right of course, the problem was in his head. Price was asked to leave after only a few weeks of this, whether out into the world or to a psychiatrist's couch no one knew.

I said, "I hadn't thought about Dwayne Price in years."

"Good. Just don't think I'm in his orbit."

"Why do you say that?"

"With all that's happened, you might believe it."

"Crazy? Never. Though the Bishop might argue otherwise."

"Then what does that leave?"

"A prankster, maybe."

He smiled. "God's the prankster, not me."

"If only I could believe that, Marbury."

"You have to. It's true."

I sipped my coffee and reviewed my notes again. The story of the accident just kept coming back to me, and I ran it over and over in my mind. A few moments on either side might have changed everything. Marbury might never have stopped and driven himself into real trouble, or he could have spent the evening in Pittsburgh, had a nice dinner and gone to bed early. But he didn't. He took a choice that he made and turned it into something else, a weird kind of event that he was invited to participate in.

"Tell me again why you didn't stop."

Marbury shrugged. "I just didn't."

"I'm wondering why you would drive right into the teeth of danger."

"Oh, that wasn't dangerous."

"Freezing to death wasn't dangerous?"

"It wasn't if you were already dead. I felt that way, you know."

But there was still the trip, he said, and his journey to Pennsylvania he tried to plan as a way to recharge old batteries. He would drive, for one, time to think and see things, time to slow down too, if only for a few days. But threats of an impending storm changed all that, and Marbury soon found himself frantic again, racing against the clock. Exactly the place that he didn't want to be.

"Meeting that little girl changed everything," he said.

"Yes, I'm curious about that. Was it a miracle or mere coincidence?"

"A bit of both."

"Well, surely, you're not suggesting—"

"And why not?"

"It's absurd. Children don't heal."

"That's what I thought."

Marbury explained that the snow at the accident was getting worse, a full-blown blizzard. Visibility was down to zero. The wind became even stronger he said, whipping up drifts and carrying them across the road, the same road where the Bronco and police cruiser struggled to cross. Wheels spun helplessly, and it was only by traveling single file, with the Bronco as the point vehicle, that they made it. The village of Wheelersburg, so small that the town owned only one snowplow, was completely paralyzed. Every store was closed. And the lone Main Street traffic light blinked on and off to itself. Not a soul was seen, walking or even in the houses. Everything looked deserted.

Thankfully the town had a hospital, or what passed as one. The building was old, built in the Eisenhower era, when coal flowed more abundantly in these parts than it did now. The town was larger too, said Marbury, three times its present size, and the decision to build a hospital should have signaled better times but it didn't. Coal was just starting to be imported from other countries, Canada and Brazil mostly, which undercut the prices. Mines shut down. Children left for college never to return. And soon Wheelersburg became little more than a ghost town. Now a ghost town in a blizzard.

The Bronco arrived first. Marbury saw a nurse and two other men waiting at the loading dock, another relic from those old days. Both the truck and emergency-room entrances were one, sharing the same door, which doubled for freight and stretchers. One of the men took the little girl and handed her to the nurse, no wheelchair, for the snow was too deep, while the other one worked on the bleeding woman. A few moments passed and he was still working.

Marbury followed the police cruiser into the parking lot and drove as far as he could to the front entrance. Then he got out. It was still snowing.

A window rolled down in the cruiser.

"You shouldn't park there, Father. You'll get stuck."

"I'll only be an hour or so," replied Marbury.

"An hour in this weather is like a week. Good luck then."

And the police drove off.

Marbury walked into the front lobby, a dreary place with green walls and nothing on them but paint chipping to the floor. He explained to the receptionist who he was and the scene of the accident that he had just witnessed, but she just shrugged ignorance and pointed him in the direction of the emergency room to wait. The lobby there was deserted as well, as though nobody was working or even around. Marbury went up to the desk and banged on a bell. No response. So he sat on an old chair that sagged in the middle and read magazines, waiting for someone, anyone, to appear. But they didn't. He said that he must have waited into the dinner hour, wet and already exhausted, and his empty stomach was readying him to leave when another man approached.

The man said, "You must be the priest. They told me you were here."

Marbury said that he was.

"The name's Barris, Jacob Barris. Like in the Bible."

The man thrust out a hand. It was like shaking the hand, bony and cold, of the dead.

"That was my wife you found out there."

"I'm very sorry," said Marbury.

The only thing that he could say really, or the exact thing that Barris expected him to say, for he responded with a kind of resigned shrug. Marbury described Barris as an angular man, thin, with a face shrunken into his skull. His cheekbones were ruddy and protruding with spider veins, as many old people's were, and his hair flew up in a great tuft, all gray and frizzy. Marbury said that Barris had the peculiar habit of blinking his left eye while he talked, as though he was struggling to keep it open.

"Maybe he had something in it," I said, interrupting him.

"And maybe he'd had a stroke. Anyway, it gave me the creeps."

"My beard gives you the creeps."

"Only because you can't grow one," grinned Marbury.

I brushed off his cheap wit. "How long did you sit there?"

"Hours. I felt like I was waiting in line for purgatory."

Marbury said that they just sat there, these two men, in silence. They didn't read, they didn't talk or anything, they just sat. Every so often an alarm would go off and the intercom would blare out a physician's name, but no doctor ever walked by. Barris started to nod off but caught himself before actually falling asleep. His head bobbed up and down like one of those old dolls found on dashboards, except one with a broken spring in its neck.

Finally the sound of shoes. A doctor. Barris arched himself upright.

The doctor was young and looked like he was already working on through his sleep. Five o'clock shadow. A stethoscope dangled in his hand.

He said, "First the good news. Your daughter is fine. Not a scratch on her body. I couldn't believe it, wouldn't have, given the impact, but there it is."

Barris shifted in his seat. "Stepdaughter. The kid isn't mine."

"Well, she's fine regardless. If you wish to see her—"

"And Helen?"

The doctor looked at Marbury. "Are you the family priest? Because if you are, she could use one now."

Barris stood up just then and demanded, "I want to see her."

The doctor put up an argument at first, but then agreed. He led the two men back behind the main emergency-room doors and through a skinny hallway. A few of the rooms were occupied, though most were empty. A good thing, for only about half the staff made it in through the storm. Marbury could see everyone pitching in, from the janitors helping with bedpans to the nurses busy folding linens. But none of them looked at them as they walked by, not knowing themselves what to expect.

In the last room was Helen, who had taken a turn for the worse. No miracle anymore, she was just lying there, the blood and gashes all wiped off and nicely bandaged. Marbury noticed several machines hooked up to her, machines that ran and circulated fluid into her veins, another that pumped her heart and blood oxygen, which beeped at irregular intervals. The beeps weren't very strong.

The doctor said, "We're trying to keep her alive. But I must tell you, every minute on these machines lowers her chances of survival. And they're plenty low now. Do you understand me, Mr. Barris?"

"You mean, she's a vegetable?"

"What I'm saying is that it may not matter."

"But she'll recover."

"Not likely."

Barris dropped to the nearest chair, stunned. He looked at his wife but she was opaque, with the same kind of pallor found in department-store mannequins. Not alive at any rate.

The doctor again:

"If you have any family concerns, you might want to address them."

"Concerns, what sort of concerns?"

"Religious preferences."

The doctor glanced at Marbury, as if on cue.

Barris said, "I'm not a religious man. No, sir. Anything but that."

"Understood. Then I'll be checking up on your wife's progress. In the meantime, if there's anything I can do—"

"There is something. I need flowers, doc. Roses. Can't be sick without flowers."

The doctor began to state the obvious, that it was impossible with the snow, but then he thought better of it.

He just said, "I'll try my best."

"Red ones, doc. White just stinks of death."

Marbury took a break from the story to reach for his coffee. This gave me a chance to catch up on my own notes, detailing Marbury's story for my records. It also gave me the opportunity to glance again at my map, which was still draped over my knees, the western part of Pennsylvania hanging down at my ankles. I ran a finger from Pittsburgh on out to Altoona and then back again, in a circle, but each time I came up empty.

"Just curious, Marbury. I'm having trouble placing your town."

He leaned over and tilted his head next to mine. The map was of the highest detail. And yet each time I looked through the jumble of towns and state forests, rivers, and reservoirs, I couldn't find it. No mysterious Wheelersburg anywhere.

"It's there. Look harder," he said.

"I am looking."

He pointed. "Try over there."

I looked but found nothing.

"You're sure of the name."

"What am I, an idiot?"

"You might have been confused, that's all. Maybe you still are."

❦

Marbury's eyes burned through me. "Damn maps anyway."

And with that Marbury stood up and stretched his body. I folded up the map, proving my point, since all along I knew of no town like the one Marbury had described. Although I couldn't jettison his story entirely. On the days that he was gone, that first week of December, snow did hit parts of Pennsylvania, though not in the amounts that he said. A few towns admitted to a few inches, others as much as half a foot or more. Still others recorded only sunshine that week, throwing everything out of whack. Nobody could agree.

When I mentioned this to Marbury, he didn't seem surprised.

"Who can predict mountains? Snow on one side, rain on the other."

In Pittsburgh, the *Post-Gazette* mentioned exactly that. Parts of the city had freezing rain, while other parts had snow wet enough to drop power lines and cause disruptions. One man, on the front page of the December 4 edition, had a snowman built in his yard by neighborhood kids, though only ten or so miles away, people complained of sewers icing up in the rain. But this wasn't so unusual. Snow was notorious for spreading itself out unevenly, especially when crossing large bodies of water or the mountains. A sudden squall could have hit Wheelersburg or whatever town Marbury claimed to have actually been in, paralyzed it even, it was possible, except that I had no record of it.

I had no record of anything.

Marbury sensed my dilemma. "Try the local paper."

"If they're not on a map, I don't think they'll have a newspaper."

"They had a hospital."

"Which is odd. A town not on the map with a hospital."

"You make this sound like Atlantis or something."

I just smiled.

"Well, then try the operator," said Marbury. "Chamber of Commerce."

Again, I already had.

"Give me the phone. I'll call."

I detected more than a hint of irony in Marbury's words, the delicious way that he stretched them out, stringing finger to hand one by one. A part of me, indeed a perverse part, wanted to oblige him and hand him a telephone just to gauge his reaction. But I didn't. Marbury was silent and he kept it that way, despite the strain his silence must have caused. He never deviated from his role. I spoke, and he replied in sign language. Nothing came out of his mouth. Not even a grunt. So total was his discipline that I began to feel that he had been silent all of his life, born that way, brought up that way. Except for one thing.

I knew that it wasn't so.

The Marbury that I remembered hated silence. He went to great lengths to avoid it, playing music, reading aloud, or surrounding himself with conversation. He was one of those individuals who couldn't walk into a room without turning on a television or radio. There was always a background of static to him, music blasting or other such diversion, which only made this current rendition of Marbury all the more puzzling. Somehow he rearranged his entire past and turned it upside down. A fact that wasn't lost on him.

"Maybe that's why it happened," he said. "God wanted to shut me up."

Silence, like the Trappist monks. Only this silence, Marbury insisted, wasn't self-imposed but delivered to him. He came back from Pennsylvania with only a fragment of his voice left. He could whisper at least, barely audible but a whisper nonetheless. The doctors, believing this voice loss to be an extreme form of laryngitis, thought the problem would solve itself. But it didn't. Failing like an old car battery, Marbury's vocal cords became weaker and weaker. He tried cutting back on his conversations, the few that he had, and started to horde his remaining words, like a miser his gold, but

❧

something always came out. A mistaken "I feel fine" or other such inanity, comments that ordinary people wouldn't think twice about, but with each slip there was one less word for Marbury to utter.

Then one morning, inexplicably, Marbury woke up with almost full command of his voice again. He didn't say anything to the doctors, and hardly even acknowledged it to himself. He just sat and watched television, wondering when to speak. The TV room of the hospital where he was staying was cramped, and nobody hung out there. Except for Marbury, who got tired of his own room and wanted to ambulate. This particular day it was full of people, some in wheelchairs, others just pushing around IVs, and maybe that threw him off. Somebody asked about the Vikings score and Marbury, without thinking twice, said only two words. They won. Clear as a bell those words except that they were the last he ever spoke.

That was five months ago.

He said, "You can't imagine it, Peter. It's like swimming in mud. I kick my feet, move my arms, but I'm not going anywhere."

The doctors who reexamined him, which included specialists from the Mayo Clinic, were all stumped. More tests were run and repeated again to determine this sudden outburst, but they turned up inconclusive. Of course nothing was ruled out. Throat specialists and oncologists were consulted about tumors and cancerous lesions that might have attached themselves to his vocal cords, even neurologists were called in to examine Marbury's brain. Again, nothing. Marbury appeared as normal, except that he wasn't. When he opened his mouth, nothing came out but a faint gasp. No words, not even a growling of tonsils against tissue.

The doctors started to give up after that. Or rather, they handed his case off to other specialists, psychiatrists mostly, and language therapists who worked on strengthening Marbury's use of sign language, which he discovered after abandoning the cumbersome tablets and chalkboards he used at first. But in the end, everyone was at a loss. That Marbury didn't speak was obvious, and the psychi-

❦

atrists, searching for some explanation other than a mystical one, offered the best diagnosis they could.

Unexplained sensory deficit due to trauma.

"I explained it," said Marbury. "They just didn't want to believe it."

"Maybe it was you who didn't want to believe. They're doctors, Marbury."

"Well, it's not unexplained."

"Some folks consider God a poor explanation."

Despite the fact that I couldn't locate Wheelersburg, or even locate snow in the amounts that Marbury had described, snow was still dominating his story. Already there was a foot on the ground, and Marbury could see that he was stuck, along with the rest of the hospital staff. He had little hope of being plowed out, at least until the snow stopped, and he tried to make the best of a bad situation.

"Why didn't you call?" I asked. "You could have notified someone."

"I don't know. I guess I didn't think I'd be missed."

"That doesn't sound like you, Marbury."

"Then maybe I wanted to be missing. Ask your shrinks."

Marbury took another sip from his coffee and turned away from me. I could have written more into this than just what he said. But I didn't. I knew the pressure he was under at the shelter, always looking for money, the entire operation resting on his shoulders. It was a normal reaction, rebellion. And I gave him that leeway.

"What ever happened to the little girl? Was she all right?"

He turned to me and smiled. "Depends on how you look at it."

Marbury said that he left Barris asleep in a chair in Helen's room. It was just about then that he thought about the little girl himself, replaying in his mind what happened at the accident scene, or what didn't happen. Helen was now worse than ever, being kept alive only by machines. Her chances for a full recovery were dwindling with the hours, and Marbury began to feel for the little girl, a child on the verge of losing her mother.

A janitor outside the door was sweeping when Marbury walked out. Marbury told him about the girl, describing her as best he could given the few minutes that he spent with her. But the janitor just stopped him.

He said, "You're talking about Miss Lucy."

"Then you know her?"

"Sure. She's a re-pat. Repeat patient. Shoot, I'll bet you she's been here twenty times if she's been here once. Down in her same room, she is."

And he directed Marbury down the hall.

Marbury walked up to a nurse's station and glanced over the desk. Nobody was there, and the files on all the admitted patients had been left unguarded. He was halfway through the pile when a woman's voice interrupted him.

She said, "I'd call security but they're out shoveling. So I guess you're left with me."

He turned to find a nurse standing there. She held up her arms like a boxer, except a boxer in pink surgical scrubs.

"I took karate at the Y, mister."

Marbury surrendered and took a step back.

He said, "No, I'm looking for someone. Lucy Barris. I was told—"

"Franklin. Her name is Franklin."

"I found her at the accident."

Her arms went down, replaced by a smile.

"You must be the priest. Sorry, Father, we get all kinds. I'm Abigail."

Marbury shook her hand and introduced himself formally. He told her all about his trip, leaving from Minnesota, and about the snow starting, and how he found Lucy and her mother on the road.

"Lucky someone found them," she said. "The police didn't always shut down those roads, you know. But they started after a guy ran off the mountain a few years back. Same place. It's weird."

"Well, they were lucky not to be killed."

"Oh, I wouldn't call it luck. Lucy especially. In all my years of working here, Father, she takes the cake."

"How so?"

"I can't explain it. I don't think anybody can. She's been in here for injuries that I wouldn't wish on a four-year-old. Broken arms, facial lacerations, bruised kidneys. Horrible stuff. Her homelife isn't what it could be."

"You're suggesting—?"

"Nobody knows. They've talked to the stepfather but—"

Her voice trailed away.

"—it's a small town, Father."

"No town should be that small," said Marbury.

"This one is. Anyway, the injuries are only half the story."

"What do you mean?"

"She doesn't stay very long. Doesn't have to. I saw Lucy with a broken collarbone once. Two days later she was healed. I wouldn't have believed it myself if I hadn't see the X rays. But it's happened before. Cuts that seal overnight, you name it."

She picked up the file on Lucy and opened it.

"Headfirst into a guardrail and nothing. It isn't right, I tell you."

"Nothing about this is right. I suppose you've heard about the mother."

Abigail nodded. "She isn't doing well."

"Will she make it?"

"I doubt it. But the girl—"

"I think it's a coincidence, Abigail. Plain and simple coincidence."

"Coincidence doesn't heal broken bones, Father. Only God does that."

I caught up with my notes right as Marbury was taking a break. He stood up again and walked past me over to a window, which he cracked. The fresh spring air crept in, a bit cool for me but Marbury liked it.

He just stood there, taking it all in. This was his first Easter at this church, his first Easter at any congregation in more than eight years. At the shelter they celebrated of course, with a meal that Marbury helped cook himself and a few readings from the Bible. But this was the first time in years that he had the opportunity to experience it with people in their own homes.

"I've been invited to six houses for Easter dinner. Six, imagine that."

"And how will you choose?" I asked him.

"Oh, I won't. I mean, I couldn't."

"You should go somewhere, Marbury. Not all of us are so lucky."

He looked at me and frowned. "What about your mother's?"

"I'm afraid she died last year."

"I didn't know that. I'm sorry."

I just shrugged. "She wasn't the same after Dad passed. Nobody was. Anyway, I have my work."

Marbury peered at me with a suspicious eye.

He said, "Damn thing to work on Easter. Especially your job."

"Well, you could make it easier on me. Stop your shenanigans."

"What are you talking about?"

"You know exactly. No more healing. No more sign language."

"I see. Is there anything else?"

"Yes. You'll have to leave here for good."

Marbury closed the window with a slam.

He said, "I can't leave. I belong here."

"Then you risk it all, Marbury."

Marbury walked back to where I had my notes and sat down. He picked up a couple of letters and started reading what I had. I could have stopped him, pulled them away from him, but I didn't.

He stopped himself instead. "Have you ever felt blessed?"

"I can't really distinguish blessing from blind fortune. I'm sorry."

"Too bad. Then you'll never know."

Marbury handed me back the pile of letters and smiled.

He said, "I've risked it all before, Peter. I guess I'll have to again."

It was quiet after that.

Marbury, who was now obviously intent on my cornering him, finding out the exact thing that I would be forced to use against him, just sat there. He didn't seem worried or even angry, unlike me. All I could imagine was anger. Anger that I was assigned to this job, anger that Marbury wouldn't listen to me or talk like a reasonable man. And I hated him for it.

But I tried not to show it. Instead I rearranged my notes, working backwards from the story in Wheelersburg. Marbury just watched me, with some delight I might add, even picking up the notes that fell on the floor.

Finally he broke the silence.

❦

"I lost family too, you know. My brother."

"What brother?"

"Rick, he died in Vietnam. Not a day goes by without me thinking of him."

"I thought you were an only child. You told me that."

"I told you a lot of things. I had to."

"You mean you told me bullshit," I said.

"I couldn't tell you the truth, Peter. It might have landed me in jail."

"For what? Lying?"

"You don't remember the letters, do you?"

I sat there for a moment like an idiot. The letters.

"—from prison."

And then it started to come back to me. His correspondence.

In seminary, Marbury was always getting these strange letters. They were postmarked from a correctional facility located somewhere in upstate New York, as I recall. I had always assumed back then that Marbury was corresponding with some anonymous inmate, as a form of prison ministry, and he did nothing to dissuade me from thinking that way.

I said, "You mean, your prisoner friend."

Marbury nodded. "The man in those letters knew my father."

"He knew him? How?"

"They shared a cell together for almost a year."

"What are you talking about?"

"A prison cell, Peter. My father was in prison."

The shock must have been etched on my face, for Marbury smiled.

"See, I couldn't tell you."

The sound of my stammering.

"Your own father? Why didn't you say something?"

"I was ashamed. Ashamed of myself really."

I just shook my head, not knowing what to say. What could

one say? We had our stories about Marbury in seminary but nothing like this.

"What—?"

"What was he in for? It's OK. People should be curious. Manslaughter, he was in for manslaughter. But cancer got him before he could get paroled."

I tapped my pen against the leather of my briefcase several times, creating this rhythm for me to think. Manslaughter. A nicer word for murder perhaps, though just as deadly.

"And how do I know you're telling me the truth now?" I asked.

"I have nothing to lie about anymore. Check it out, you'll see."

Marbury leaned back and glanced away from me. He seemed embarrassed, not just about his father but about steering me toward the awful truth. Prison life. I couldn't imagine my own father there, or any father of the men that I went to seminary with. Our lives were all so ordinary compared to this, and I told that to Marbury.

"Another reason I said nothing. I sound like a Dickens novel."

I nodded, thinking about all those days of incarceration. It must be horrible to be trapped with nothing but time and memories, and I told him that.

Marbury agreed. "But that's not the worst of it," he said. "My father was innocent."

"You know this for certain?"

"Of course."

"But to know for sure—"

"I would have to have been there, yes."

Somebody walked into the church at that moment, interrupting us. I tended to my cold coffee and thought about what Marbury was telling me, strange stories from both ends of our history together. Then and now. The thought of Marbury concealing that story about his father and then lying about it actually disturbed me. I considered us close at one time, and I shared with him many of my intimate dreams and fears. And I thought he'd done the same.

I had more questions about the incident but I could see that Marbury was busy. It was late and I started to pack up, my intrusion here being apparent. Marbury didn't notice. He was talking to a young woman at the front of the church who was obviously deaf and quite shaken. I could see her hands moving but I could only make out half of what she was saying.

And then I heard it. A baby.

I saw Marbury peek under a red Indian blanket that the woman was holding and smile. The baby started to cry again. Not the crying of a hungry child or even one who was tired, for I've heard my brother's kids, but a sick child. The woman was now frantic. I saw her hands moving, pleading, and I reached for my glasses. She was telling Marbury that her baby wasn't right, I could see that, that the baby cried for hours on end often without consolation. And now she faced another fear, that the child was just like herself. Deaf. A neighbor tried pots and pans, she said, but no response. And now she was worried why God would do such a thing, whether God even cared. Worse, whether there even was a God to care.

I watched Marbury closely. He bent over the child, pulled back the blanket, and kissed its forehead. Nothing else. The woman cried and hugged him, and Marbury told her that everything was secure in God's hands. That she shouldn't worry. That everything would be the way that God intended. And then he said one other thing that haunts me even now.

He said, abandon yourself to God.

Marbury saw me watching him as he came back. He fell into the seat next to me, knowing full well that I had witnessed everything, and he said, "I didn't know what else to say."

"You should have told her to go to a doctor. That child might be sick."

"Some folks don't trust doctors."

❦

"And they trust you?"

"They trust God, Peter. I'm nothing."

"This is exactly what I'm talking about. Do this and you won't last."

Marbury peered at me. "Are you telling me that a priest can't pray?"

"I'm telling you that you can't heal people."

He smiled and gurgled some more. Laughter.

"Con men and road show preachers heal," I said. "Not priests."

I tossed the notes into my briefcase, punctuating my point. Marbury just sat there and stared at me, making me feel uncomfortable. He was right that a priest ought to be able to pray for healing, but I couldn't admit that. Not now. Not under these circumstances.

"You set up false expectations, Marbury."

"I don't. I never said I could heal. I didn't even suggest it."

"Then why would anyone say it of you?"

Marbury just shrugged. "I guess because of Pennsylvania."

I sat down again, for in my rush of anger I had stood up.

"What the hell happened to you out there anyway? Tell me."

"I found God, Peter."

"God?"

"It's amazing what you can find in a blizzard."

Marbury said that the snow was getting worse in Wheelersburg, now a full-fledged emergency. Everything was shut down. There were reports on the radio that the National Guard was being mobilized, though nobody could confirm that. When Marbury looked outside, he couldn't see how anyone could mobilize in this kind of weather, military or otherwise. The snow was now well over a foot deep and still coming downward. The sky and the ground matched perfectly, absolute whiteout conditions, and nothing moved, except for the power lines that swayed in the wind and threatened only darkness.

Fears of losing power aside, the hospital readied its emergency procedures. Meals were brought out of storage. Electric generators and batteries were brought up to speed, should they be needed, and special operating rooms set up for any incoming. Somebody called over to the town hall about the snowplow but only got a recording. It was just sitting there anyway, stuck in the snow like every other vehicle, and the hopes of being cleared out anytime soon evaporated after that. They were stuck.

Marbury pitched in where he could. He spent the evening delivering coffee to the staff, and even did a bit of shoveling. Abigail, the night nurse, saw Marbury working on the loading bay, which had more snow falling from the concrete overhang. He was almost waist deep in it but he tried to shovel it anyway, intent on clearing a route for future emergency vehicles.

"Forget it," said Abigail. "Folks are on their own in this weather. We couldn't save anyone if we had to, Father. The roads are all closed."

Marbury asked her if she heard any updates from the radio.

"It's pretty grim. Another foot, maybe more."

"I'll never get out of here," he said.

"You'll get out. It just might take a while."

Marbury stuffed the shovel into the nearest snowbank and kicked the ice from his feet. No boots. He was cold and it was almost morning, though the sky looked the same old puffy white, hardly brighter.

"How's Lucy?"

"About time for my rounds if you want to come."

"I'd like that," he said. "What about Helen?"

"Still on the machines."

Marbury took off the coat that he'd borrowed from an EMS worker and slipped it back in the fellow's locker. He'd never know.

They walked down the hall to Abigail's station, where she picked up her clipboard and the few things that she would need on her rounds. A blood-pressure cuff, for one, child's size, and they went to Lucy's room.

"Who's Franklin?" asked Marbury. "You said her name was Franklin."

"That was the mother's name. I guess the stepfather wanted nothing to do with the child, since it wasn't his."

"And the birth father?"

"None. No records anyway. You see that a lot in hospitals. We get more immaculate conceptions than even you guys. Women without boyfriends or husbands. Hear them talk and you'd swear it was God."

Abigail walked through the door first. She flipped on a light and went over to the bed where the child was sleeping. Marbury looked at Lucy closely. She had dark hair, which was shoulder length, that curled up around her neck and onto her pillow. Her nose was small, like that of a pug, and matched her face. Baby fat. She looked younger than her four years.

"I have to take your blood pressure, Lucy. Stay asleep if you want."

But the girl just rubbed her eyes. "Is that you, God?"

Abigail glanced at Marbury and smiled. "See what I mean?"

Marbury didn't pay any attention to someone waking up, especially waking up in a room as gloomy as this one. Gray walls, no window. No pictures. Hardly even a bed. It looked like a room in a penitentiary.

"I remember you," said Lucy, cracking her eyes. "Terrible accident."

"This is Jim Marbury. He's a priest."

The sound of ripping Velcro. Her blood pressure was normal.

"How are you feeling?" asked Marbury.

"Bad boo-boo." And she rubbed her head.

"Your head hurts?"

"My head, and Mommy's head. She's sleeping with the angels now."

The nurse glanced at Marbury and frowned. Not far from the truth.

Marbury said, "You're right. Your mommy's very sick. Now you have to pray, Lucy. We're all praying."

"But I'm not allowed to pray."

"Who says?"

"Jacob. Jacob's mean to God, but God isn't mean back."

"Then we'll keep it as our little secret. How's that?"

"Secrets are fun as long as you don't tell."

Marbury watched me write, scribbling things down as fast as I could. I wasn't going to take notes, but I did anyway, a habit of mine, and this time was no exception. While I scrambled to catch up, Marbury had left and brought us back a few beers that he had stashed somewhere, and he opened them up. I took a long swallow.

He said, "I heard Rinker's burned down."

Rinker's. It was an old seminary bar where we sometimes snuck away to. Hardly more than a neighborhood hangout in Decorah, Rinker's had a jukebox and that kept us sane. Plus talking or watching sports on the TV.

I said, "That place was a firetrap. Probably electrical, eh?"

"Not this time. A woman came in with a can of gasoline and torched the place. She said her husband was spending too much time there with his girlfriend."

"Good riddance then."

Marbury smiled and worked his beer.

He thought for a moment, then said, "Do you ever miss it?"

"Rinker's?"

"No, I mean out there. Do you ever miss it?"

❦

Out there.

I set down my notes and looked at him. Marbury was using those words but he didn't mean them. Those were just words behind the words. He was really talking about something else. Something we both knew but were afraid to acknowledge, that many priests were afraid to acknowledge.

He was talking about sex.

I thought about it too, and just like Marbury I often used another word to describe it, though in the end it was still sex. Creeping middle age hasn't slowed these thoughts either—not that I'm sure I want them slowed. Like slowing up a part of life. Even celibate I could still feel. I had to feel, for it was only by feeling that I could fight off the very temptations that gnawed at me, that sent every other temptation running for cover. The temptation for peace. A home, a wife, a family.

Not that I was perfect. It was the sixties and I grew up like every other boy, stealing pictures of Marilyn Monroe and Anita Ekberg from my mother's movie magazines, then taping them inside my locker at school. When I hit sixteen, I decided on the real thing. A girlfriend. And I found the perfect one. Her name was Molly. She was a sheepish-looking girl with great, thick bifocals. As far as I knew, Molly had few other friends, which only made her the more accessible to me. I tried with the other girls in school, the cheerleaders and musical types, but I never seemed to get anywhere with them, which only pushed me back to Molly. She gave of herself freely, ending my own adolescent torment one night in the back of my parents' station wagon, a Country Squire. It was roomy and spacious, this car, especially constructed in Detroit—I was convinced of it—for exactly such encounters.

It's strange, but even now I still think about her. The eyes that squinted when she took off her glasses like some cartoon caricature. The fumbling, nervous way that she undressed, cautious and fearful, for she had much to fear. A predator takes his carrion any way that he could get it, and I was no exception. I preyed on Molly for the worst of all possible reasons, because she was willing.

Marbury looked at me and grinned. "I'm human. I know I do—miss it."

"Do you ever think about marriage?"

"Sometimes. But then I remember my vows. I'm pledged to God."

"Pledged or just flirting?"

"No, it's the old ball and chain with me now."

Marbury's humor I took in stride. In seminary I remember him as a man who walked around like he had the world by the tail. That he was once involved with women, probably a great number of women, nobody would deny. But he wasn't the Lothario that we all expected. Marbury wasn't the first one to talk to any woman who happened by, whether visiting family or friends, and he didn't seem twinged with that same kind of desperation that affected many of us. Whether wrestling with our sexual identity as some did, or just wrestling with the notion that sex was a part of the world, Marbury never seemed touched by the struggle. He was comfortable with his celibacy, almost relieved by it, as though he was pleased to give it up.

I only saw him waver one time in those years. It was our last autumn together. Marbury was nowhere to be found, spending most of his time, I discovered later, volunteering at a hospice for the terminally ill in Des Moines. I didn't consider this out of the ordinary for him. He was fascinated by death and dying, and he always wanted to work with people suffering what people had to suffer in life. But who he really wanted to work with, I think, at least I think this in retrospect, was the director of the hospice.

She was a striking woman with dark eyes and hair, who was just a few years out of college herself. She radiated a youthful charm and ebullience that Marbury gravitated to, as she in turn gravitated to him. I saw them together only once, by accident, when I was visiting a friend's mother who was dying of cancer. I saw Marbury there and he introduced us. She mentioned that she had heard all about me, that Marbury kept her up on the gossip and tidbits of our seminary and that she felt like we had already met. We had dinner together that night and I could see how they talked. Not the talk of ordinary people casting off words like trash, but the talk of two people in complete harmony with one another.

She struck me as Marbury's perfect woman. Tough enough to handle him and what the world had to offer, yet tender. I myself would have carted them both off to the chapel, married them on the spot if I could have, had Marbury not been in seminary. In the end, though, it wasn't meant to be. Despite the perfume wafting from Marbury's clothes, he denied that he was interested in her. And when she walked down the aisle with another man less than a year later, Marbury viewed it as a vindication. But I knew better. I knew it was love renounced.

When I asked him if he remembered her, Marbury just smiled.

He said, "She got married. I should remember that."

"That could have been you."

"But it wasn't. She wanted me to leave, you know."

"Why didn't you?"

"The priesthood was my home."

"Do you still feel that way."

"More than ever. I love my life here, Peter."

I looked at Marbury and I envied him. He was given everything good that the world had to offer. Intelligence and charm, a beautiful woman who adored him, and he gave it all up because he loved what he was doing more.

I said, "I don't know if you're crazy or content, Marbury."

"Some of both, like always."

And with that Marbury walked me to the door and saw me out.

He waved to me as I went to my car, the cool evening air wrapping itself around my body and urging me to go home.

But I didn't listen.

A duplex on the north side of town.

Her voice. "Well, you know she was deaf too."

I shut the door behind me. The lock clicked.

"A lot of my friends, the auxiliary mostly, they were all surprised. She didn't act like it. I think she read lips. Just like on television, only you had to talk slower."

My voice. "How long did she live here?"

"Almost three years."

"And she just pulled up and left?"

"I just rent rooms. A mother I ain't."

The landlady, a short woman dressed in a bathrobe and pink slippers, led me past the foyer to the stairs. The smell of bratwurst cooking in the oven wafted by me and brought back memories of a place that I lived at in college. Another boardinghouse much like this one. Same kind of woman too. Old but feisty.

I looked at the stairs. They were steep.

"No, in here."

She pointed to a door on my right. I opened it and we walked in. It was a simple room with a bed, nicely made with a fresh quilt, and a chest of drawers, plus a small writing desk. I examined a few of the drawers, pulling them out, hoping for something, an address or a letter, some indication of where the tenant might have gone, but they were all empty.

"What about her mail?" I asked.

"Don't know. Never came here. Forget about kin either."

Another loner. Marbury always seemed to heal only loners.

I ran my finger across the bed, just thinking.

"Did she have any problems getting in or out?"

"I don't ask, they don't tell. But she could move about fine."

"What about the wheelchair?"

"She had a cane too, Father."

"A cane? I thought she couldn't walk. I was told—"

"Well, she walked right out of here. Vamoosed."

"She actually walked?"

"Not very fast. Not that I can walk fast at my age."

I couldn't believe it. I didn't believe it.

"Sounds like a miracle," I said. "A woman leaving her wheel-chair."

But the landlady just huffed, skeptically.

She said, "The real miracle is that I got paid. She never paid up."

"You don't find this unusual?"

"Walking? Nah. Now heal this and you got yourself a real miracle."

The landlady showed me her hands, both of which were horribly swollen. Broken veins popped out, all blue and distressed looking.

She said, "Hurts so bad I want to chop one off except that I might need it someday to chop off the other. They go in pairs, you know."

"I'm sorry. I wish I could help."

"You mean, you don't heal?"

I shook my head.

"I thought that's why you were here. To sign me up for Sunday."

"What's happening Sunday?"

"It's Easter. Nobody feels pain on Easter."

"Who said that?"

"Your man."

I was beginning to feel stupid. "You mean Jesus?"

"No, the guy who heals. He's having a special service, you know."

And then I understood. Marbury.

She said, "Just hold a spot for me, Father. That's all I ask. I simply can't live with these hands anymore."

MAUNDY THURSDAY.

The next morning I found myself sitting in the Bishop's office, filling him in on what I already had. I told him more about the accident and the result of that, as well as the few personal revelations about Marbury's father, which I spent the evening confirming. Everything checked out, exactly the way Marbury said. His father was in prison for several years in the late sixties, sentenced for manslaughter but he never made it to parole.

I also told the Bishop about my conversation with the landlady and the search for someone actually healed by Marbury. But I didn't tell him about the baby. I couldn't. Not without being absolutely certain about Marbury's motives.

The Bishop sighed. "Is that it? Nothing else?"

I said that it was. He just peered at me as though he had X-ray vision.

"So what you're saying is that you haven't told him yet."

"I wanted to see where he was going first."

"You know where he's going. Your boy Marbury thinks he can heal."

"It can't be that cut-and-dry. Something happened out there, Tony."

"Sure, something happened. He found God. Lord save us all."

I just sat there, feeling stupid. But it was my own fault. I could have just filed my report and left this business unfinished. Except that this was Jim Marbury. I owed him the extra yard. I owed him more than that.

"So when are you planning to tell him?"

"Soon," I said. "I'll tell him soon."

᪗

"Myself, I would have opened with that."

"He deserves a chance to clear himself."

"You're giving him a chance. Just don't fumble it first."

Marbury was sitting in one of the pews when I walked in, busy with a large, silver bowl. He was polishing it, rubbing a slow cloth into the metal grooves of its design and then using his breath to wipe it clean. I watched him for a bit before he noticed and waved.

"I thought I'd wash some feet tonight. Maundy Thursday."

I dropped my briefcase next to him. "What, no Last Supper?"

"Soup and bread. You're welcome."

"I have feet too."

Marbury smiled. "Forget it."

I watched him work. He polished the bowl as though he was going to put it in a museum. Hardly his purpose. This was a vessel of complete humility. But Marbury would have none of that, humility. He washed others' feet because Christ washed them first.

"Are you expecting a good turnout for Sunday?"

Marbury nodded. "But Good Friday I expect more. I'm told that's the big day around here."

Good Friday. Nobody attended church in my family on that day. We saved everything instead for Easter Sunday. I remember fighting my three other brothers for the bathroom to get ready. We brushed our teeth, combed otherwise unkempt hair, and put on suits, a rare thing for a kid. Easter was, in our farmhouse in Minnesota, a celebration of spring, as pagan as that sounds, for the long winter had finally ended. But it was more than that. It was a chance for egg hunts and chocolate rabbits, and a chance to gather with the family, uncles and aunts included, and eat.

But church came first. It was always crammed, and it took an extra fifteen minutes or so just to seat everyone. The chatter was like birds with kids crawling beneath pews, jabbering, throwing paper airplanes constructed from the freshly crayoned pictures of Jesus made only a few minutes earlier. Then the sermon. More fidgeting, more pinching and weird looks. A couple of parents cleared their throats, powerless, for nobody wanted to scold their children on Easter and we all knew it. Finally, after what always seemed like a thousand years, the service ended with a triumphant ringing of the bell and everyone ran out, the kids at least, playing and chasing each other until our parents caught up.

It was fun.

I told this to Marbury expecting to hear a similar such tale from him. But I didn't. He said, "Easter wasn't one of my favorites. I lost my mother on Easter."

He turned away from me and when we finally locked eyes again I offered my condolences, years late.

"What's to be sorry for? People die. It's the cornerstone of our hope."

"Living is the cornerstone, Marbury. Living, not death."

He smiled. "Yes, yes, you're right."

Marbury explained to me that it was his mother's death that really gave him his first real experience with the church. He was fourteen. Breast cancer had ravaged his mother's body, forcing her to bed for long periods of time. Just when the end seemed near, death imminent, Marbury's mother would rise out of bed again and go back to her normal life.

"Almost like Lazarus," he said.

Marbury said that his mother would do her best making everything in the house seem ordinary. She would put on her beloved Motown records and dance when she could. Other times she cooked and did laundry. She never spoke about death. She never even mentioned her illness. But after a few days of this she would end up back in bed, sicker than before and the whole waiting game would start right again. Gradually the house grew darker as her spells in bed became longer and longer. Curtains were left drawn and remained that way until she died.

"What about a doctor?" I asked. "Surgery must have been an option."

Marbury shook his head. "She was a Christian Scientist. We had an elder pray over her a few times, but as for real physicians—"

His voice trailed off, or rather the sign language.

"And your father? Was he around?"

"Oh, he was around. He just said we shouldn't cry."

Marbury stared ahead for a moment. His eyes looked distant, as if he were in another world from this one.

Finally he said, "We were robots, my brother and I. Right on through the funeral. I guess the old man felt guilty or else he had enough with the Scientists; either way he returned to the church of his youth after that, which was Catholic."

But this death, said Marbury, like so many changes in life, only signaled more turmoil. First came the end of his father's job. A tile salesman, Marbury's father had managed to keep the family together and relatively content with this one job. But shortly after the funeral, his company went bankrupt. Severance checks bounced and the pension that he was promised went to Switzerland, smuggled out of the country in some other guy's pocket.

Money was tight after that, said Marbury. And his father, unable to secure anything better, took the only job he could find. A janitorial position in an office building. He was to keep the place clean, or try to. A nearly impossible task with five floors of restrooms and hallways of tracked-in mud, snow, and rain. But he tried anyway. Months went by. The money, never as good as the old sales job, ran out faster. The family tried to consolidate of course, by moving to a cheaper apartment, then by selling the family car. But these were only short-term plugs in a dike leaking from bad luck. His father knew that and tried to keep a step ahead, moving every few months to increasingly cheaper and cheaper apartments, ever cheaper until down to the marrow and bone he cut.

Meanwhile bill collectors started to call. Threatening notices were posted, evictions, late-night repossessions. Marbury said that his father picked up other jobs at neighboring office buildings. More toilets. More carpets to vacuum. Saturdays became Sundays. Days became nights. But his father rarely complained, telling his children that despite their apparent string of bad luck, everyone could achieve their dreams if they just had enough faith.

"This doesn't sound like a man who would end up in jail," I said.

Marbury looked at me and agreed.

He said, "I think he really believed it too. Then Rick died."

Rick Marbury was the oldest brother. According to Marbury, he was a bright student with dreams of going to college. He was accepted at NYU, an incredible reversal of luck for the family, and they celebrated one night at a local burger place. That's where events turned. A man in a wheelchair sat across from them, obviously a veteran. He was sitting with two other men, also just home from the war, and they were discussing their experiences in Vietnam. It was the first time that Rick had ever seen a real veteran up close, much less someone injured from combat, and it brought the war home to him for the first time.

He said, "It bothered him. Rick thought we should be doing more."

It was 1965 and one of the first offensives was in full swing. Every night the boys watched the war on television. They watched the helicopters swoop down, the way the grass spread out and flattened against the heels of rushing soldiers, and they were transfixed. Better than *Gunsmoke*, better even than a John Wayne movie, the war was the real thing. And the more he watched, the more Rick started to feel the call. He began to wear army jackets and fatigues.

Then one day, out of the clear blue, he responded the only way that he could. He enlisted.

He was only nineteen.

Vietnam affected my family as well but I didn't tell Marbury that. Two of my brothers went, and I only remember not picking up a paper back then, not even the sports page. And I never turned on the news. If I heard anything about the war, I walked away immediately. I just couldn't think about it until my brothers were home safe.

Marbury snapped his fingers. Like napalm.

He said, "You're not writing."

I couldn't.

"How many of us joined because of Vietnam?" I asked.

"A few."

"Come on. Half of us maybe."

"Half believed, half didn't."

An image suddenly came to mind but it wasn't Vietnam. I was thinking about seminary and an event that happened while I was there. Something about belief.

"Do you remember the bell tower?" I asked Marbury.

He nodded. "Dave Karl. You're really digging in the past now."

The bell tower was one of the more beautiful buildings on our campus. It was brought over, piece by piece, by stonemasons from Italy who constructed it to honor God and a promise to new life in America. Every hour the bell chimed, a wonderful sound, though today I couldn't hear it without thinking of Dave Karl.

Where he came from, no one knew. It was said that he was a star pupil from some California school or perhaps even home educated. But that was only speculation. Karl appeared to us, and ultimately left, with more questions than he answered. I met him my first year. I was in search of a role model and I found one, Dave

Karl. He was a bright student, almost meteoric, with an infectious energy that led even the worst of us, slackers at best, to become an army of dedicated workers. He organized food drives for the poor, outreach ministries, counseling, even ministry at summer homes and cabins. Wherever there seemed a need, Dave Karl was there to fill it.

And people helped. I myself offered freely the use of my time because I knew that Karl would somehow get it done. Whatever the task. I had faith in his abilities as a priest and as a man. All traits that I felt held real promise. Honesty, integrity, a sense of quiet righteousness. In retrospect this promise was exactly that, a promise for something paid in funds not yet earned. For only three months after I met him, Dave Karl was gone. A suicide, he was found hanging by the rope of his cincture in the bell tower. Dead.

"They pulled him out in front of me," said Marbury. "He was blue. All puffed up like a fish."

I later heard that there was a note, pinned to his body at the time of his death. It just said that he couldn't live up to the expectations anymore, others', much less his own. In reality, I don't think that was true. He just couldn't live with himself. For stories started to come out. Disturbing tales about trips to massage parlors in Minneapolis and Chicago, tawdry visits to street hookers and sex houses. Rumors began to float about what was found in his room after his death. Ads for phone sex, boxes of illicit photographs of young men and women, films and magazines. And all of this was damning.

A few students, however, including his closest friend, tried to reclaim the image of Saint Karl, or resurrect a new one better to their liking. They claimed that the discovery of these materials only proved that Karl was working on a new project, an outreach program for sex workers, and that he was merely educating himself to that world. But I didn't buy it. Neither did the police who checked out his phone records. Apparently all sorts of calls were made, some

❦

hours long, and when they were traced back to the source in Los Angeles, several of the women who spoke with Karl remembered him by his peculiar predilection. They called him the spanker.

But this wasn't the end of Dave Karl. A few months later, a fellow was walking by the bell tower one night when he saw someone standing up there. Curious, he walked up a rickety set of stairs, the only way up, and claimed to have found no one. And the myth was born. The ghost of Dave Karl was responsible for everything after that, from the occasional missed chime to water dripping from the bell on clear days. Even today they still talk about the ghost, and the bell tower, now nicknamed "Karl's Tower" for the new students who look up there and just wonder why he did it.

Me, I was past wondering.

I looked at Marbury and said, "He was a coward. He conned everyone into thinking something about him that wasn't true."

"I don't know about that. He did some good."

"You couldn't stand him."

"I couldn't stand him because I was jealous."

"Are you still? I mean, you're beginning to sound like him."

Marbury arched his body back in the pew and smiled.

He said, "I think you should resign yourself to the fact of my fate. I have. The way I see it, the Bishop has no other choice."

"You're not giving him one. Understand his dilemma. If he sanctions that you can heal, that God took your voice in some mysterious snowstorm, then he sanctions divine intervention. That God picked you out individually for this. Next, folks will be praying in your name."

"The hell with that. You know what they did to Theresa. Ripped her body up for relics."

"I don't think it'll go that far, Marbury. Sainthood."

"Neither did she." He smiled.

But I wasn't amused. "Do you wish to remain a priest?"

"I'll still be a priest, Peter. No matter what you do."

"You'll be a man who calls himself a priest. A big difference."

Marbury looked at me. His eyes almost burned with anger.

"Why are you here? You don't want the truth, Peter, unless it's easy."

I was offended. My whole spiritual life was a quest for the truth, no matter the form, and I told him so. But Marbury just shook his head, wagging it, as though mocking me.

"Your spiritual life is based on reason, Peter. Don't part from that."

I protested, "You're wrong."

"Am I? Then explain to me why you ran that night."

Marbury's memory was astounding.

What he was talking about was a story that I only told him once, and yet it must have made an impression, for he still remembered it. We lived in those days just outside of a small town called Pennock. Hardly even a town, certainly not more than a stop on the highway, Pennock was a feed store and a bar. Little else. My father met my mother, a Norwegian, right before the war and they married. They were given a piece of land out there from my uncle, less than a hundred miles from Minneapolis, and my father, having no career of his own at the time when the war ended, decided to give it a year to see if he liked it. That was 1946.

I was born on that farm, along with one of my brothers and my sister, Sandra, and our childhood revolved around farm life. Work was plentiful. There were animals to feed, crops to be planted and harvested, and school, which meant an old one roomer, only a few miles up the gravel road from our house. I had to walk to school and back every day and night, and I was doing exactly that when it happened.

I was ten. It was winter and the night was cold, well below zero. The sky was electric with stars and I dawdled as I walked. I kicked a chunk of ice down our long road, thinking that I was Gordie Howe probably, my feet crunching the frozen snow with every step. Maybe I didn't notice the light behind me or maybe I suddenly turned around, I don't know. All I remember is seeing it. Like a flashlight beam hanging in the sky.

At first I thought it was lightning but I didn't hear any sounds. It was quiet, like maybe a comet or the northern lights, except brighter and smaller. I just stood there and watched it. Then a funny thing happened. I noticed that the light wasn't just hanging there, it was moving. And moving toward me. I watched it some more to see if it was a plane, but I couldn't hear anything. No engines, no distant rumbling. Nothing at all. The light, as I watched it, appeared to be getting closer, much lower in elevation than I thought. And it was getting brighter, a stronger beam that started to illuminate objects on the ground, mounds of snow, mostly, the odd standing cornstalk, and finally, me.

My fear got the best of me, this being the late fifties, and I started to run. I kept thinking about the movies of Martians and flying saucers that I saw, huge crafts with death beams and robots attacking earth, and I started to pick up the pace. But it was terribly icy and I found myself slipping and falling. The light didn't stop. It was closing in on me, focused now only on me, and I started to run wildly, off the road and through the fields, where the snow was even deeper. I tried to zigzag away from the light, which was at my heels, but I couldn't shake it.

My house was straight ahead, a few hundred yards away, and I ran faster, picking up my knees through the snow, but that only made me tire quicker. The light was closing in, presumably to suck me away, vaporize me or whatever aliens did, and I was running for my life. Then it happened. I stepped in a ditch or something, a huge drift at any rate, and the snow was up past my waist. I was stuck. The light flickered around me. I couldn't see the stars anymore. I couldn't see anything but my own death.

❦

"Then what?"

I looked at Marbury and shrugged. "It just veered away and left."

I told my family about the light, I even inquired about whether anyone had seen it. But they hadn't. I don't even think they believed me. Certainly not my brothers, who tortured me after that. They left cardboard aliens on my bed at night, and walked in while I was sleeping with flashlights against their faces, whooping and yelling. After a while, I began to doubt the story myself. None of the big papers, from Alexandria to Saint Cloud, had even a hint of a UFO encounter in them, if indeed this was one, and I found no one to confirm that anything unusual happened. Despite the early hour of the evening, despite the fact that someone had to be driving home, there were no witnesses, no reports at all except for mine.

"I lived but it wasn't easy. I was a laughingstock for a while."

"What do you think it was?" asked Marbury.

"I don't know."

"But you saw something."

"Maybe it was a military plane."

"And maybe it was something else."

"It was probably nothing," I said.

"So you ran away from nothing?"

"I was a kid, Marbury." I heard my voice rise a few decibels.

"Why didn't you hold your ground? Weren't you curious?"

"More like I was afraid."

Marbury shook his head violently.

He said, "No, you ran because you couldn't explain it. You ran to protect your little world, not because you were afraid of something unknown in the sky but because of something unknown inside of yourself, Peter."

A part of Marbury was right but I didn't tell him that. Instead I tried to steer the conversation back to a place where I was more comfortable, back to Marbury's story.

I said, "The same could be said of you. That you ran."

My face felt flush. I could feel the anger starting to well up.

Marbury smiled. "Is that what you really think?"

"The police found your car in New York. Explain that."

"Maybe it was stolen."

"From a town I couldn't find on a map? Come on."

"I didn't run, I assure you that."

"But the car—"

"Well, I wasn't driving it."

"It didn't drive itself, Marbury."

He shrugged. "Then I guess we do have something in common, Peter. The unexplainable."

We just sat there in silence after that.

Maybe Marbury didn't know that I was aware of what happened to his car to begin with or maybe he didn't have anything else to add. I don't know. But he didn't seem to be too concerned about it. The car, his beloved old Cadillac, was found by the New York City Police Department and later towed away, and Marbury knew nothing about it. Whether it was stolen or Marbury simply drove it there himself, no one knew. He certainly didn't have it when he was found in Altoona, days after the accident, just walking the streets with only a long-sleeved shirt on. No hat, no gloves, no coat even, despite its being winter. He must have looked homeless out there; or worse, he must have looked mad.

I had just finished with my notes when I heard something, a loud growling from the pit of Marbury's stomach. It sounded like a human earthquake.

I asked him, "Are you going to make it?"

He shook his head. "Not unless I get some food. I'm starved."

Marbury suggested breakfast at the diner across the street and I agreed. We stopped in his office first, a small cube wrecked by an apparent storm of books. They were everywhere and heaped in the most inconvenient of places. There were books serving as doorstops, stacked on radiators and chairs, on windowsills and on couches. There were even books propping up other books. I looked around for a place to sit, but I finally gave up, realizing that dispersing one pile would only create a second, even more precarious one. It was a strange sight, Marbury surrounded by books. He didn't like reading, and in seminary he was famous for giving away every book he had except for a few. And those he never looked at.

"Where did these come from?"

Marbury was changing his clothes in the bathroom right behind me. He walked back in, standing now in a white oxford shirt like any ordinary citizen, and shrugged.

"The last guy. I guess he was in a hurry."

He tucked in the tail of his shirt and just stood there. For an instant I considered taking off my clerical collar as well, but I couldn't. It didn't feel right.

Marbury sensed my dilemma.

He said, "If I don't take it off, I'll hear confession with my eggs."

"Sometimes that's the job, Marbury."

"Sure, but do I have to starve doing it?"

We ended up walking out of the church into the brisk, spring air. The diner, a gloomy place just off of Lyndale Avenue, looked like it was out of a bad episode of TV. The place was small and cramped, with dim-lit booths decorated in red and green check. And the floor had a thin sheen of grease on it, a bad sign, I thought, for it covered everything else, including my new black shoes. I gave Marbury a look of disgust but he only grinned.

"I know what you're thinking, Peter. But it's really delicious."

I found that hard to believe but plunked my body in the booth anyway. Food was still left on our table, half eaten, and our waitress, a thin blonde dressed in a skirt too tight for her body, came over to clear it.

❦

The sound of popping gum.

"We're fresh out of hash, boys. No corned beef. Now if you want hash with just potatoes and onions that's another story."

I glanced at the specials but avoided them. Finally I settled on an omelet and toast, plus coffee, black without cream. I made a point of this. Marbury set down his menu and signed his order to me, which I promptly relayed to our waitress. It took her a moment to make sense of this exchange.

Finally her voice.

"Oh, my God, he's deaf."

"Actually his hearing is just fine."

"You mean—? Not even a word?"

"Not even a peep."

She just shook her head and walked away, trying to absorb it. I commented to Marbury about her shock but reminded him that he had to expect some of this.

"Act different and you'll be different," I said.

"I'm not acting. I really can't speak."

"Then we'll try other doctors, Marbury. I'll talk to the Bishop."

"You mean shrinks. No thanks."

"You can't choose to live this way. I don't accept it."

And I didn't.

But Marbury just shook his head. "You don't have to."

Then he added:

"It's my life, Peter. I finally got it back and I'm going to keep it."

The waitress brought out a pot of coffee just then and left it there, along with a fistful of cream and sugar. Marbury made his usual production, which I had completely forgotten about over the years. He pulled out two bags, shook them, and slowly sprinkled them into his coffee, tasting it along the way. Eventually both bags would

make it into his cup but not first without a process. Marbury dribbled the sugar in as though each few granules were enough to make
a difference, then he would stir, far longer than necessary. A thin
tinkle of spoon and ceramic.

Finally it was perfect.

I just drank mine and settled in as Marbury elaborated about
getting back his life. He said that the snowstorm in Wheelersburg
was the final straw, and he recognized that his whole existence before
the trip had a wild frenzy to it, motion without a center. And he
vowed to correct it, change everything in his life, once he came back
to Minneapolis. But Minneapolis was a long way off.

I interrupted him. "Did that include your ministry?"

"Yes, if need be. I was tired, Peter."

"You could have taken some time off. A vacation might—"

"I didn't need a vacation."

"Then what?"

"New skin. I wanted a new life I guess."

"And I suppose you found that in Pennsylvania."

Marbury just shook his head.

He said, "No, in Pennsylvania I found the old life, only recycled."

Pennsylvania.

A voice in Marbury's ear.

"That bench, not exactly the Holiday Inn."

It was the janitor standing over him, holding a push broom.
Marbury, exhausted from driving and the events in the snowstorm,
stretched out on the nearest thing that he could find and fell asleep.
And now he felt like he was waking up from the dead.

"What time is it?" asked Marbury, light rushing into his eyes.

"Late, later. But it's still snowing," said the janitor.

Marbury sat up to take a look for himself but he couldn't see

❦

anything. The window was completely iced over with frost about an inch thick. It looked impenetrable.

The janitor peered. "You'll have to take my word on it."

"Are we plowed out yet?"

"Better chance on finding the ark, Father."

"But I have to leave."

"We all have to go somewhere," said the janitor. "Lucky to be here, we are, instead of out there in that thing. Except if you're Miss Lucy's mother."

"Why, what happened?

"It ain't looking so hot."

Marbury excused himself and walked down the hall to Helen's room. During the night several more machines were added and now were hooked up to her body, beeping and running out a long line of graph paper.

Barris was still in his chair, head slumped, his hands folded over the back of his neck as though he were expecting mortar fire. Marbury walked in, past the vase of red roses the doctor had delivered, and knelt down.

"What the hell good is that?" It was Barris.

"Sometimes God intercedes," said Marbury.

"God—?"

Barris stood up, almost whirling, and pounded the closest table with his fist. Marbury thought that it was going to shatter but it didn't.

"—I'll tell you about your blasted God. I've done enough for him. And look where it's got me. Did everything I was told to, I did. Helen said it would work out. Promised it would, but your God ain't dying on some table, now is he?"

"There's still hope."

"Hope? You sound like that fool child."

"You're talking about your daughter, Jacob."

"My daughter—?" He laughed.

"You're her father, like it or not."

"I'm not her father. I'm just a stand-in. Like the other guy."

"What other guy?"

"The last stiff, Joseph. Read your Good Book, man."

Marbury didn't know what to say. And for a moment he thought that the stress of his wife's injury was just too much for Barris. That he was losing his mind from grief.

But on the contrary, Barris was crystal clear.

He said, "Yeah, Joseph and Mary, you heard me right. He had to be talked into it too, except that nobody knows what happened to him when the action got started. You never read about that. There's no Joseph hanging around at the feet of Jesus, now is there? He's gone. Where I should be. Wonder why that child is sitting there with hardly a scratch? I'll tell you. Because I'm not the father. He is." And he pointed to a crucifix over the bed.

"You mean God?"

"Who else?" Barris said, "Helen's no spring chicken, padre. Doesn't take a genius to put together two and two. She's well over fifty, despite her looks. But the seeds were all dry at forty. A proven fact. Go ask her doctor. I just married her. The truth is, no man would have her but me. Not that there isn't love, I'll admit my love."

I interrupted Marbury at that point and said, "This is insane."

"That's what I thought."

"You mean, he was actually convinced that God fathered his child?"

"To him it was Gospel."

Marbury said that Barris told him the story of how it happened. It was almost five years ago.

Barris explained that Helen drove out to his farm one day to give him a freshly baked pie. But that wasn't the only gift she had. They knew each other, and Barris once rebuilt her family's leaky roof and every so often she would drop off a pie out of thanks.

Usually it was around Christmas. But this time she came by a few months earlier, impelled by a dream that she had that told her to go to a farm with lots of broken machinery lying around, and the only place that she could think of was owned by Jacob Barris.

Barris had already heard the scoop. That Helen was pregnant, well over seven months by now, and that nobody knew the father. He was shocked like everyone else. Helen was seen as something of a spinster in town, never married, and she devoted much of her time to the church. Her father had left her some money, not a fortune but just enough to live on, and she spent most of her day baking meals or quilting, with the proceeds going to the poor. Everyone considered her a religious woman, virtuous and moral, at least until she got pregnant.

"Then all hell broke loose," said Barris, "as you can imagine. Nobody believed it when she said that she was a virgin. They called my Helen every name from slut on down."

"But you believed her?" asked Marbury.

"I didn't have a choice. I mean, I thought it was hooey, a crock of you know what. But something happened. Hell, I can say it. I felt the baby kick. Put my hand right there, I did. Now I've never been one for children before, but seeing that foot just reeled me in like a mud river catfish in spring. Ever feel a baby kick before?"

Marbury said that he hadn't.

"A hell of a thing. Got me right here."

But Barris caught his tenderness before he got carried away.

He said, "But that's how the bastard works. A cheater he is, letting my Helen rot here. I did what I was supposed to, I took in the little brat. Helen promised me that this time it would be different. No dying on a cross or any other way."

Barris stood over his wife and tears began to well up.

And one last time he said:

"God's a traitor, padre. I'd kill him, I tell you that. I'd kill him already, if he wasn't God."

• • •

The waitress came by with our food, interrupting the story. I set down the notes that I had been working on and watched Marbury, who dug into his ham and eggs with gusto, the same voracious appetite that he had in seminary. He was always a good eater, albeit not a very healthy one. Marbury seemed to exist on nutritional fumes, living on such delicacies as pizza, doughnuts, and soft drinks. In seminary he was always the first in line at dinner as well, eating his fair share and always flaunting his appetite, in an Aunt Bee kind of way, to the other students who pecked and plucked at their food as though it were birdseed.

"Jesus didn't starve," he told anyone who would listen, "so why should we? There's little virtue in hunger, you know."

Not that Marbury was a glutton. He didn't blow up, grow fat like one of those old Roman emperors. The opposite was probably true. The more Marbury ate, the thinner he actually became. Some of this I attribute to his running. Not jogging but track, he called it, back in 1971. Marbury was the first person I ever knew who ran for entertainment. After class, he would don his gray sweatpants and sneakers, nothing high-tech in those days, no Lycra, no expensive running shoes, and he would jog out into the countryside. Sometimes he ran for hours and returned so exhausted that I almost feared he couldn't eat. But that fear never materialized.

"So how is it?" I asked.

"Good. Better my voice than my tastebuds."

I smiled. As for my own food, it didn't taste extraordinary or even all that different from any other omelet I've ever had. That was the big contrast between Marbury and myself. In sensual matters he devoured like a child, always a first time for him, his eyes open with great excitement and anticipation compared to my old tried and true method, which wasn't a method at all. It was just living.

"Have a chunk," he said.

❦

A piece of ham, a river of dripping grease, hung from Marbury's fork like a downed suspension bridge. I tried to decline the best I could.

"What are you, abstaining from meat now?"

"I'm just trying to be sensible. I don't have your build, Marbury."

He looked at my plate and frowned. "You have to eat something."

"Don't you ever worry about cholesterol?"

"God made cholesterol too, you know."

Marbury didn't change. In some ways he was still the same man who begged our cooks in seminary to make meat loafs and sausages, anything with meat in them, which only infuriated people. There was a movement, popular then, of vegetarian dishes, often only clumps of green kelp or spinach, and fresh bread. These were our staples, vegetables and bread, not the Texas-style cookouts that Marbury would have preferred.

Some people took exception even to vegetables. There was one seminarian who insisted on eating only ovum; that is to say, he ate exactly that which presumably could be harvested and consumed without killing the host specimen. Mostly he ate nuts and fruit. Other vegetables like broccoli, potatoes, and carrots, anything that had to be uprooted or chopped off, killed, were excluded on moral grounds, namely trading one life for another, which this fellow considered immoral. It was a bizarre philosophy and not one without its opponents, Marbury for one, who thought the idea downright insane.

He said, "We live by killing. As for Creation, it'll be redeemed later when the prey meets the lion. In the meantime, Peter, have a slice of ham."

And I found it on my plate.

Our waitress came by to freshen up the coffee. She kept glancing at Marbury while she exchanged a warm pot for the one that we had all but drained. He told me to thank her for the meal, which I did.

She leaned into me and with a quieter than normal voice said:

"I saw the Helen Keller story. Plain horrible."

"You don't have to whisper," I said. "My friend already knows that he can't speak. He assumes everyone else does as well."

"Does he——?"

"Accept it? Yes."

"You poor man," said the waitress, studying Marbury. "How do you sing?"

Marbury gave me a look, which I returned in kind.

"He doesn't," I said.

"Criminal, not to sing."

The waitress just shrugged her shoulders and walked away. She didn't have to deal with Marbury's story. For her, Marbury was simply a man who lost his voice. But for me the story was more than that. It was both an explanation of where he had been and a signpost to where he was going. And I didn't like either one.

Marbury looked at me. At times he could almost read my mind, and this was one of them. He was sensing my doubt.

He said, "You don't believe it could happen again."

I knew exactly what he was talking about. Another Christ Child.

"Could, yes. Won't, more likely."

"But the Resurrection——"

"Risen, Marbury. Not an encore performance."

"It sounds like you've already made up your mind then."

"I have." My voice was firm.

Marbury nodded and forced a great heap of scrambled eggs into his mouth. He ate without a care in the world, as though he was confident that everything would work out. A confidence that I didn't necessarily share.

Reinforcing this, I said, "You're not helping any. This story—"

"I know it's unbelievable."

"I'm glad you agree. How do I bring this back to the Bishop? He already has my future in his pocket from the last time that I helped you and brought you here."

"Why did you do that?"

"It's my job, Marbury."

"I thought this was your job, snooping around other people's lives."

"Your welfare is my job. You might not believe this, but I want you to succeed. I want you to shine."

"But on your terms."

"On everyone's terms. Don't be selfish."

I knew that would rattle Marbury and it did.

He said, "I don't work in an office, do I, Peter? I'm out in the world."

A low blow but one that I probably deserved. I didn't start out thinking that I would end up in an office either, but after almost fifteen years of it, it's a job that I've come to respect and I told Marbury that.

He just nodded his head, saying nothing. It's not that I haven't thought of other positions or even held the job descriptions in my hand. Rather I just felt better suited for this one. That's what I told myself at least.

Now I even questioned that.

"Tell me what to do with this story, Marbury."

He just raised his eyebrows in surprise.

Marbury said, "You just write, Peter. Then let God do the rest."

I bristled at his use of God again. God the giver, the protector of life, and like Shiva in the Hindu scriptures, God the destroyer as well.

I said, "Unfortunately, God won't decide your fate. The Diocese will."

He laughed, making me feel stupid.

"—You know what I mean."

"Yes, yes. You could relieve me of my duties."

"I could relieve you of everything you've worked so hard for."

Marbury looked at me and smiled.

He said, "I think I'll take my chances with God."

Marbury stuffed another piece of ham into his mouth, followed by a quick bite of jellied toast. Had he been able to speak or even wished to, I'm sure that he would have been humming to himself by now, a smug reaction to my authority. And I couldn't blame him. The truth was, I was going to listen to his story regardless, he already knew that, and despite my doubtful reactions to the contrary, I was still perplexed by his story enough to hear more.

That there were elements here of a collegiate prank, I couldn't deny. And I often felt that at any minute a gang of our old friends, including the Bishop himself, would just jump out from behind the scenery and begin the inevitable ribbing. They would tease me about how gullible I was and we would all have a good laugh. Except that when I looked around I saw no one but Marbury.

He glanced down at my plate and asked me if I was going to finish my toast. I told him to go right ahead, which he did. Both pieces.

"Never waste, Peter. I've seen too much hunger."

"At the shelter?"

He nodded. "And growing up."

"Why didn't you just get a job yourself? You could have helped out."

"Only a farmer's son would ask that. I did get a job. Later."

Marbury said that Rick, his brother, was in Vietnam only four months before he was killed. The news hit the father like a brick. He quit his job as a janitor and settled on a new path, drinking all day and watching the soaps. The family went on welfare and lived on food stamps, which Marbury traded in for cash so his father could drink. They gave blood together, sold scrap aluminum and stolen car parts. Anything for drinking money. This slide would have continued, said Marbury, probably right into cirrhosis of the liver or worse if not for one thing.

Graduation.

He was now almost seventeen, a senior in high school, and Marbury was thinking about what to do with his life. He had all but ruled out college. No money for it, much less any ambition. And this left only one other path in his mind. The military. But his father didn't like that.

"He already lost one son. He wasn't about to lose a second."

"What did he do?"

"He got a job. Quit drinking right there."

Albany was a tough town back then. And the neighborhood numbers were run out of a local bar that Marbury said his father would occasionally frequent. He got to know the place, its customers, and the business that was conducted there, and he cleaned himself up for a job. He took a position first as a runner, then at records until finally working himself all the way up to payoff man. The profits were good, and soon Marbury said that his father heard the most delicious sound at that time. The jingle of change in his pocket. Bills were paid and money was being set aside for his father's dream, of Marbury one day attending college.

Marbury said that he started to come to the bar as well, just to wait for his dad. After work they would go out and get a burger together and discuss the day. They kept no secrets. Marbury knew what his father was doing and he didn't blame him. He just let it go. As the weeks passed, Marbury said that he found himself lingering in the bar longer and longer, waiting for his father, who always was busy. He found himself watching more TV, drinking and eating the free peanuts and soda, killing time mostly until it suddenly came to him. Something bigger than himself.

"They had a pool table," he said. "Big thing. Green as money."

And so Marbury taught himself to play.

He took books from the public library and started to read about the great pool sharks. Guys like Minnesota Fats and Willie Mosconi. Marbury began to practice new shots as well. Angles and tricks, sliders and hooks. He shot pool until his arms ached and then he shot some more. Somewhere along the line he became very good.

"I could beat anyone who walked through the door. And that was my problem. I felt like I could never lose."

It was a problem as well because business for Marbury's father began to take a turn for the worse. Betting had begun to slide into the same recession that everyone else was feeling, and along with a renewed crackdown by the police, folks started to stay away. Money got tight. The middlemen demanded more, cuts were passed around that left less for the retailer, the guy at the bottom. Marbury said that his father, now a full-fledged bookie, began to work even longer hours to make up the revenue. Fourteen-, sixteen-hour days. He covered the spreads on everything imaginable from elections to basketball, even European soccer. But the profits still shriveled and before he knew it, the slide backward resumed.

"That's when I heard the call of the stick," said Marbury.

"You played for money?"

"I played to survive."

There was a whole psychology to master, a psychology that, Marbury said in retrospect, seemed to match his adolescent leanings to a tee. A pool shark had to be arrogant but still vulnerable enough to be beaten. The easiest way to do this, what Marbury called the loudmouthed approach, was to overstate one's ability in public. This always involved money and the notion that the opponent was being hustled, badly hustled as it were. Marbury would select his prey and start the act, saying how good he was, that he couldn't be beaten, et cetera. Then he would shoot around the table, not playing his best, for this was the double blind of pool sharking. No two opponents ever knew each other's real strengths until it was too late.

Somebody would suggest a small fee, maybe five dollars a game, and the balls were racked. The first few games Marbury would lose terribly, throwing more money into the pot, swearing and grumbling to himself. Eventually the ante would be raised. Twenty bucks a game or maybe more. And the opponent, if he was good, used a kind of counter psychology found only in pool halls. He held back as well, perhaps even throwing a game just to crank up the ante. Marbury, using a counter to the second counter, had to appear to play his best, pulling out all the stops until he won. Then of course, he would take his money and start to leave.

That's when the real game began.

The opponent, sensing that he could really win, would finagle a last, winner-take-all contest, which reluctantly, almost kicking his feet, Marbury would agree to. And the slaughter would begin. Marbury would launch every reserve he had, and if he had calculated correctly, he would beat the poor individual into submission. If he hadn't, then it was his Waterloo. He would get destroyed.

With this method, Marbury said that he earned several hundred dollars a week. But it wasn't always that easy. Sometimes the betting never escalated past the five- and ten-dollar range, and he would gain very little for his efforts. Other times, the opposite would happen and bids would rise quickly with his opponent throwing in dollar after dollar until he was cleaned out. The saddest thing to watch, said Marbury, for people rarely knew their limits, especially when it came to their egos.

"So what you're saying, Marbury, is that you were a crook."

"That's not a word I would necessarily choose."

"What then? Hustler, confidence man, scam artist? You pick it."

" 'Entertainer' sounds better. I liked to entertain."

"And do you still?"

Marbury gave me a lazy smile. "I haven't entertained in years."

Our waitress returned with more sugar for Marbury, who had already used up every packet on the table. I thought that she'd returned just to take another look at him, as though Marbury were on display somewhere, but I was wrong. That was reserved for me. She fixated this time on the clerical collar that I was wearing and ran her eyes up and down my body, not solicitously but with a hardened, studious kind of gaze.

More popping gum.

She said, "I dated a priest once. He could see women. Go out."

"A pastor, you mean. Protestant."

"All I know is that he dated women. I mean he wasn't—"

"Celibate?"

"God, no." And then she laughed.

Her laughter sparked something within me, the memory of a recurring dream that I often had. In it, I'm being led up to the gates where Saint Peter, a clean-shaven man dressed in a black Armani suit and shirt, presides over eternity. He's sitting at a desk full of huge ledgers and scrolls, and he's busy making notes, just scribbling like mad.

I'm standing there, naked, no clothes to speak of, certainly none of my official black, and old Peter doesn't know whether I'm alive or dead. He just keeps on going about his business with the ledgers and such, quite busy, and he moves from ledger to ledger, always writing. I let him scribble some more, then clearing my throat I announce myself.

Peter Whitmore, I say.

But the old apostle doesn't even look up, he's so busy. I announce myself a second and a third time. Then I do something that surprises me, even in the dream. I grab Peter's hand. He stops and looks at me and I can see into his ledgers by now, which are completely blank. He's writing but nothing is going on the page.

I'm a priest, I say with pride.

And old Pete just bursts out laughing. And he just keeps on laughing until I wake up in a cold sweat.

Marbury had heard this dream before. I had it in seminary a few times and I told it to him, but he didn't see any significance in it, then or now.

He just said, "People laugh. Both in dreams and in real life."

I watched our waitress circulate around another table. She probably had a whole routine down, talking to people, probing their inner workings, and then moving on. Like a game.

"Anyway, it's just your imagination. More likely your fears."

"How is it, Marbury, that when Helen has a dream about finding a husband for her child you lend it credence, while my dream says nothing?"

"Don't be insulted."

"I just don't understand it."

"It's a stupid dream, Peter. That's all."

"Maybe Helen's dream was the stupid one."

He shook his head. "I don't think so."

Marbury went on to explain why. He said that one of the nurses from the hospital in Wheelersburg, apparently suffering from nicotine withdrawal, braved the snow to retrieve an extra pack of cigarettes from her car. But the snow was deep, in large drifts, and she returned with frozen feet. Not frostbitten, though cold enough to cause her discomfort. She did her rounds anyway, limping and cursing, which continued with every patient until she reached Lucy.

Abigail was the first to notice it.

"Damnedest thing," said the nurse. "I was taking her temperature when I felt it. Like a tingling in my feet. But everything's all toasty now."

"What did she do?"

"Nothing, that's it." The nurse shrugged and walked away, recovered.

Abigail looked at Marbury and smiled. But he wasn't buying it.

He said, "She's a child, not an oil burner."

"Sure, a child of God. Something's not right with her, Father."

Marbury said that he didn't know which way Abigail meant that, and he decided to hedge his bets by looking in on the child. Lucy was in bed, half propped up by several pillows that had to be folded twice just to create enough cushion for her head. She just stared off into space. No toys, no books, no television. No place for a child at all.

He circled around the room once to make sure she was actually awake, but he still wasn't sure. Lucy didn't say anything. Marbury said that he was about to leave when he heard her voice. She said it was cold. Marbury told her about the snow, which she couldn't see, and he talked about snowmen and sledding. But Lucy just shook her head.

"No, silly, it's cold."

She held out her hand, which Marbury felt. Like ice.

"Cold boo-boo."

"You're frozen," he said, trying to warm her.

And then Marbury noticed it. A diabetic identification bracelet dangling from one of Lucy's wrists. It was so loose that had Marbury not caught it, noticed it at that very moment, it might have easily fallen off and got lost in the sheets.

"You'll need this," he said, adjusting the bracelet tighter.

She smiled a thank you and tucked her hands under the sheets for warmth. And that was the last said about it.

But Marbury couldn't let it go. He kept thinking about Lucy and her mysterious injuries, now compounded by the fact that she was diabetic. And it made him angry.

He asked her, "Do you get many boo-boos?"

"I come here. Sometimes I fall."

"How do you fall?"

"Jacob says I fall."

"Oh, Jacob says."

"Then I come here. But I get better."

"Do you fall again after that, Lucy?"

"I fall and fall. Others fall too. Lots of boo-boos."

"What happens to the boo-boos?"

"God keeps them. In his box."

"He has a box?"

"It's big and yellow. Boo-boos go in there and live."

"It must be a very big box, Lucy."

"The biggest. For all the boo-boos."

"What does Jacob think about the box?"

"Damn child."

"He actually says that?"

"Damn child. Sometimes I fall."

"And you come here."

"I get better. Every boo-boo fits. Mommy's. Jacob's. Even yours."

Marbury said that he must have given Lucy a quizzical look, for she pointed right to his chest. More exact, right to Marbury's heart.

"That one, mister. A really big boo-boo I see."

Marbury closed his eyes for a moment, breaking the thread of his story. When he opened them again, he looked far-off and exhausted, as though somehow the plug had been pulled from him. He no longer seemed the vibrant, energetic man of only a few minutes before but old and worn out, like a man aging before my very eyes.

I asked him, "Did you alert the authorities?"

"What are you talking about?"

"The man was a monster. Surely you didn't let her stay there?"

Marbury struggled a thin smile.

He said, "Barris wasn't a monster. He was just a man."

"Which means you did nothing."

"You're missing the point, Peter."

"I'm missing that you left a child where she shouldn't be."

"She was safe."

"Landing up in a hospital isn't what I call safe."

But Marbury shook his head. "You need evidence."

"Were you trying to find any?"

"Yes."

"You didn't want to get involved."

"That wasn't it. I was already involved. Don't you see?"

I felt my face get flush and my pulse was racing. Marbury looked at me, then placed his hand on my shoulder for comfort. But I didn't feel any comfort.

He said, "I was angry too. But then something happened."

When I couldn't even muster up a response Marbury added:

"God boxed up my boo-boo."

I was stunned. Marbury was past being just another priest for me, our history together, our friendship assured that, but I didn't know what to say. I was no longer just questioning the decisions that he made in Wheelersburg, I was questioning the decisions behind the decisions. His entire foundation.

But Marbury didn't care about that. He said, "Lucy was right. I had claws within me, tearing from the inside out."

"You listened to a four-year-old?"

"I listened to God. Everyone has a boo-boo, Peter. Even you."

I just shook my head.

"Don't worry about me, Marbury. I'm just fine."

"Really? Then why do I feel you bleeding?"

What Marbury said to me, or what he was even suggesting, seemed presumptuous and I told him so. My own life had nothing to do with the story of his going to Pennsylvania and his voice fluttering about in the wind somewhere supposedly speared by God for purposes unknown. He might have pulled that years ago, trying to turn the tables upside down on me as though it were my fate in question, my very happiness, but he couldn't do that now. I was older.

Marbury, who had been staring out the window while I railed away with exactly this, turned to me. His eyes twinkled again, a fresh energy surging, or maybe the thought of a good fight.

He always loved a good fight.

"All I'm saying is this. My happiness isn't a condition to be debated."

"Who said that it was?"

"You implied it. You were unhappy; now I must be too."

"Are you?"

I diced up what remained of my omelet, cutting it into smaller and ever smaller pieces until I was left with only mush. The thought of defending my own mental state to Marbury seemed absurd, and not something I wanted to pursue. The truth was, I was neither happy nor unhappy but an odd mixture of both, an idea that Marbury wouldn't understand. For him, the world was divided into two camps with no separating ground, no gray at all. And sometimes all I felt was surrounded by gray.

"I'm pleasantly content," I said.

Marbury smiled. It was the same smile that I remember from all those years ago, a smile bred from victories large and small. He liked to win, and living in those cramped seminary rooms, stifled with the many inconsiderations that we were forced to contend with, cold showers, poor food and such, battles were fought every day. Not that many of us joined him. We, I include myself as well, we endured the boiling hot classrooms, the old communion wine, the books with torn spines and covers, assuming that this was part of our newly chosen life.

But not Marbury. He spoke up, or if he didn't speak up he protested in other ways. Like the showers. Colder than the Arctic Ocean, our showers were the morning humiliation that each one of us detested but shuddered to resist. Nobody could figure out the source of the problem, cold water, whether from the plumbing or one arranged for us to overcome. Everyone complained of course, to themselves mostly, afraid that real complaints might lead to an obscure call somewhere or worse, a call to a town so small that the only showers left were cold ones.

Marbury laughed at us like sheep being led to the slaughter.

He said, "You want to blame the boiler but you shouldn't. Try Christ. He bathed in cold streams, why shouldn't you? Enjoy it, I say."

And he did.

Much to my surprise and amusement, Marbury made a game of freezing in the showers. If the water was freezing, more freezing than usual, say like the temperature of liquid hydrogen, he would complain that they were too hot. He would yell to the Father Janitor to rush down more cold water, words that I heard myself. And the Father complied. Eventually Marbury used this tactic with everything. If the soap smelled bad, as it often did, he used more. Or if the telephone was out of order he would say that he thought we should go without. The other seminarians, myself included, all thought that Marbury had lost his mind, or his will to rebel. Not that we were so brave as to demand better ourselves, cowards the whole lot. But we still fought, albeit quietly, with the contempt of a beaten dog toward his master.

Marbury observed this behavior from his perch. While we raced in and out of the showers at lightning speeds, Marbury lingered. He sang. He soaped himself languidly. He dawdled for as long as human skin allowed before turning blue or until he was told to put a move on it. It was a force of will that I later came to recognize, born from the pool hall, playing one perception against another. But it was something else. It was Marbury taking up the ultimate cross, which the rest of us spent time evading. For he loved the very thing that tortured him most, and by loving it, he transformed himself forever.

Weeks passed with this strategy. Then it happened. I was in the shower at the time, barely getting wet, when I felt it. A brief splash of warm water. It lasted for only a moment or two before surrendering back to the cold but that was enough. Hot water. Maybe this was meant to throw off Marbury, remind him that hot showers did exist somewhere in the world. I don't know. I do know that he never flinched. No reaction at all. Gradually more and more hot water arrived, especially when Marbury was showering. He just did his same old routine, singing and lingering and sometimes even yelling for more cold. Soon, I adopted his strategy as well. Others followed on cue, grinding their frozen teeth and singing until our showers began to steam over with hot water.

When I asked Marbury if he remembered this he just smiled. He said, "Don't be too impressed with that."

"Why? We had warm showers again. We won."

"If they wanted to crush us, Peter, they could. Turn off the water and people would beg for showers. Any shower."

"Even you?"

"I'd be the first one in line."

I nodded. This wasn't the Marbury of twenty years ago, the cocksure kid who froze in the shower to make a point. This was another Marbury, a compromised man. Or a man compromised by the power of God, he might say, compromised of his freedom, or the perception of his freedom, by a force larger than the sum of all things. God was in control of all that was: of darkness and light, of cold and hot, and straddling these nuances, or even worrying about them, was an exercise in futility.

I said, "Then you've changed."

"Haven't you?"

I couldn't answer that. Not honestly. For in the spirit of change I've seen people cast off their old selves with reckless abandon, shucking off skin and history in the pursuit of something new, which usually was, in Marbury's words, just the old recycled. And I was afraid of it.

"Change is natural, Peter. You can admit that."

"Leaves falling from trees, that's natural. Reversing full course—"

"And you believe that I've done that?"

"Yes."

Marbury just shook his head. "Then you don't know me very well."

Our waitress came by and cleared the dishes. She balanced everything on one arm like in the movies, holding the swaying cups and plates. I saw her scramble into the kitchen, stopping first to pour coffee for a few truckers with her free hand. One of the men, a burly fellow with a thick red beard, looked at me and stared. I stared back.

Marbury, noticing that I was watching something, turned around. The man was still staring at me, despite his friends laughing and cooing with the waitress. She slipped a long bang of blond hair behind an ear as she talked. Everyone laughed, including the man with the beard. He broke his gaze for an instant, just long enough to reach up behind her skirt and pinch her. The waitress squealed but the man only looked at me and winked.

I felt Marbury's hand.

He said, "This isn't the O.K. Corral."

"Will you look at that guy? All nerve."

"There are a million jerks like that, Peter. Try prison."

The man went back to his friends, laughing and joking. But I couldn't help thinking that I was the real butt of his joke and not the waitress.

Marbury was pouring himself yet another cup of coffee, not paying attention. He was busy playing with the new bags of sugar that our waitress left him. Stacking them up like sandbags, he built tiny walls around his coffee cup. I imagined Marbury as a child and wondered what would have happened to him had his mother never died. Another direction maybe. Another life altogether.

"You said that your father was innocent."

Marbury looked up. "How did you get all the way to there?"

"Just thinking about prison, that's all."

The man was still laughing. It was like I never existed.

"Interview ten inmates and you'll get the same story. What makes you so certain of your father's innocence?"

"Because I was there."

Marbury said that the reason his father went to prison all began with pool. It was good fun at first. He would set up shop while his father was working late, or on Saturdays. Marbury said that he hung around like a kid should, drinking soda and keeping himself clean from bad influences. No smokes. No beers. And certainly no girls. He did this to please his father, but more importantly, he did this to check out his clientele. While people drank more than they could hold, Marbury would size up the competition or watch the games already in progress. Or if no one was playing, he would rack up a set to play alone, certain to dump a few easy shots in case anyone was watching. Which they usually were. Eventually a person would take up the cue against Marbury. Money would be mentioned, then set aside for safe keeping by the bartender, and it would all begin.

Marbury said that his father kept a blind eye to the pool table, or at least if he knew that his son was playing he wasn't objecting any. Money was still trickling in and he was busier than ever, running around just to cover all the bases. And the number of clients, though not as many as in the past, proved a godsend for the young pool shark. For it meant a steady stream of people, some terrible at playing, some worse than they thought, others just fair to middling. Marbury worked these folks hard, he said, because they were his bread and butter, but also because he knew that others would work them even harder.

"I never let anyone walk away completely broke. They always had cab fare. Lunch money at the very least."

I wasn't impressed with his magnanimity.

I said, "Maybe you could have allowed someone else to win."

"I only did that once. That was enough."

It was a bright autumn day, Marbury said, and he was finishing up with someone, beating the pants off him. Marbury was tired and wanted to go home when he walked in. A sleazy hood of a man, his hair oiled back, with bushy eyebrows that tried to conceal a vicious scar over his eye but couldn't. Marbury said that he had a bad feeling from the start, an instinct about the fellow, and tried to wiggle away. But it was too late. He saw the money. Hundred-dollar bills.

There was an unspoken code in the neighborhood, a kind of ethics of pool hustling, that kept the sharks away from one another. Only one hustler per bar, that was the rule, for if the public knew that sharks were on the loose, all money would dry up, disappear completely, and nobody wanted that. Marbury said that he gave anyone who even looked suspicious a wide berth, refusing to play or even just to hit a few for he knew the consequences. A full-fledged war with all the casualties of combat.

"I guess this means you played him."

Marbury nodded.

He said, "He couldn't even hold a stick. I found out why later."

Marbury tried to get out of playing, he said, by throwing the first few games. He thought that if the man was bored, or saw that no real money would ever come of it, that he would just quit. But he didn't. In fact, the opposite happened. The more Marbury lost the more interested the man got. He threw in more money, doubling it after every win. And it didn't matter how much Marbury contributed or even whether he contributed at all, the man threw in money anyway.

"Finally it became too much. Maybe I got greedy."

Marbury, exhausted but sensing his biggest payday, started to play better. He won a few games easily and it went to his head. He started to feel invincible. Money was added to the pot, escalating the game and his ego more. Shots went back and forth, routine stuff except for one shot, a banker that left the man deep in a corner. Too deep for a left-hander, which he was, but the man tried to compensate by shifting to his right. And that's when Marbury saw it. The scam.

He was a natural right-hander.

Marbury took advantage of the next break to play his hardest, ending the game as quickly as possible, before the man had the opportunity to switch to his good side. After the eight ball was dropped Marbury reached over for the money, which wasn't left with the bartender as usual, who was in the back room resupplying, but in a plastic cup. Marbury said that he'd had enough.

A hand reached down.

"It ain't over till I say so, kid."

"I started to back away," said Marbury to me. "A bad move."

It was a bad move because the man came after him with a pool stick. Marbury, barely seventeen, quickly found himself cornered against the door of the men's room with nowhere to escape.

"Playing games, eh, kid?"

"Just pool, mister. Take the money and we'll call it even."

Marbury was scared.

"I don't fucking care about the money."

The man with the scar flashed an evil grin, along with a knife. The sort of knife that one used to clean deer and wild animals.

"Don't care about the money at all."

Marbury said that he was about to say his final prayers, kiss his life good-bye, when he saw his father, who had heard the commotion all the way in the back room.

He said, "Let the boy go, mister."

The man turned slightly, still pinning the blade into the boy's stomach.

"I'll gut this kid. You get in the way and I'll gut a second."

"I'm his father."

"Then I guess I'll have to gut you both."

The next events were sketchy. A fight ensued, the sound of pool sticks being snapped, the flash of a moving knife. Before he knew it, the three were on the floor fighting for their lives, when suddenly Marbury found himself holding the knife. Everything stopped.

The man stood up, laughing. "Got the hair to do me, kid?"

Before Marbury could answer or even think, the man with the scar over his eye lunged forward and in one motion, sheer reaction on Marbury's part, the knife moved straight into his chest, stabbing him.

"I must have severed the aorta. Anyway, he was dead."

Marbury took a sip of coffee as I just sat there. Dead.

Then he added, "He moved more than they do on television. One leg kept flopping up and down, then a minute later it didn't."

Marbury said that the wail of a police siren pierced the air. Someone from the beauty shop next door actually called the police, unusual for a betting joint, he said, which only reinforced in his mind the ferocity of the fight. While he and his father waited for the law, Marbury said that his father did a strange thing. He took the knife from his son's shaking hand and kept it. The police found it that way.

As the cops pulled him out, handcuffed and confessing to the murder, his father, Marbury said, whispered something into his ear that he never forgot.

He said, "Live a good life, Jimmy. Second chances are rare."

"I still try to remember that," said Marbury.

I felt myself slumping in the booth. The story stunned me, I'll admit it. The random horror, the sheer gruesomeness of it, struck me on many levels and I found it fantastic, like something you watch on television but discover only later happening to you in real life.

"What did they do to your father?"

"He went to prison. I wanted to tell my side of the story, the truth, but he wouldn't let me. He figured the cops would nail him one way or another."

"But if he was innocent—"

"None of us is that innocent."

I shook my head. The story was coming to me in waves, still building.

Marbury knew what I was thinking, for he said, "I killed a man."

I tried to water things down. "It was self-defense."

"Was it now?"

"You were fighting for your life, man."

❦

"I shouldn't have been there in the first place."

I didn't know what to say. The problem with relationships really. No matter the amount of empathy employed, how much human intimacy created, it was still nothing more than employed intimacy, manufactured empathy. I didn't plunge a knife into a man's chest, and I couldn't feel the horror of watching a man bleed to death in front of me, no matter how long I lived.

"Well, you were a child anyway."

Marbury smiled. "God doesn't wait for birthdays. Neither do killers."

"Surely you don't believe God was involved?"

"Not directly perhaps. He didn't take the knife."

"Then how?"

"One path ends, another begins. Everything changed after that."

Marbury said that the judge gave his father a reduced sentence after he heard about the difficulties that the family had suffered through and the fact that the murder was in self-defense, though the judge never could really buy that. In his mind gambling led to murder anyway and couldn't just be explained away with the vagaries of a street fight. So he sent Marbury's father to prison. Hard time. But soon after his arrival Marbury said that his father began to throw up blood and he was found to have stomach cancer.

"He didn't last long after that."

It suddenly hit me. "You had no family."

Marbury shook his head. Fortunately he had an aunt to live with. A woman descended from good Puritan stock, she believed that everyone should make their own way in the world, without help from anyone. But when she saw the younger Marbury the aunt couldn't help but bend her own moral rules and offer up her home, which she did.

She was a widow whose husband left her a small fortune, money that he made on Wall Street, and she lived on a small estate in

❧

Connecticut. The aunt never had any children, a good thing, said Marbury, for children wouldn't figure easily into her extended cruises and trips abroad. Not even teenagers. Marbury found himself alone in the house for months at a time. After he tired of the surroundings, the horseback riding and fishing, he found other things to occupy him. Trouble mostly. The stuff the late sixties were so famous for. But the important thing, said Marbury, was that despite the rebellion of his youth, God still left him with a choice. Prison or the priesthood, though it wasn't obvious to him at the time. It was just another path.

He said, "So I chose the other path. God's prison."

Our waitress came by holding up two pieces of cake.

Marbury looked at me, then at his watch. It was almost lunch. His eyes widened as if to tell me what he wanted without having to sign it to me.

"He'll take chocolate," I said.

She pushed the aroma with her hand. "Fresh baked. Can he still—?"

"Taste? I'm afraid so. Taste. Smell. Hear."

"Oh, God. I did it again. I'm sorry."

Marbury offered her a smile but she was too embarrassed to take it. She just left our cake on the table and walked away. Marbury shrugged.

"I seem to have that effect on people."

"You have some sort of effect. I'm just trying to figure out what."

Marbury thought I was being vague but I wasn't. Several members of his congregation that I interviewed told me that they attended church only because of Marbury, that he made them feel closer to God.

One of them said, "I've gone to maybe twenty churches since I

❦

was a kid. But nobody made me feel like I actually belonged like Father Marbury."

Another one: "I didn't like it here before. The other priests made me feel helpless, like just because I can't hear I need God more than you. They preached a good line, equality. But I never could buy it. Now I can."

Marbury listened as I read these quotes to him, his head bobbing. When I asked him for his thoughts about why people would say this, why he had struck such a nerve, he tried to brush me off.

He said, "I'm just one of the gang. Another quiet one."

"Except that you can heal. How do you do that?"

"I've told you already. I don't do anything. God does."

"But God listens to you."

"I just pray, Peter. Good old-fashioned prayer."

"And does prayer absolve sins? Or do you personally?"

He gave me a hard glance.

He said, "I pray, that's it. God deals with sin."

"Kneeling or standing?"

"What?"

"Your prayers, do you kneel or stand? Eyes open or closed? I'm interested in your methods, Marbury. If you have a key—"

"I have nothing."

He took a bite of cake as if to punctuate himself.

I just sat there and toyed with my fork. Marbury was like a stone wall. He denied or confirmed nothing, and everything was built on a fault line and could come crashing down at any moment.

"What are you fishing for, Peter?"

"You already know. No more healing. No more prayers."

"I mean, what are you really looking for?"

I was hesitant. Finally:

"The Bishop has a job for you. I'd consider it."

"Let me guess. Something with an office. Probably a tiny one."

"You can work behind the scenes."

❦

"You mean, I can work where nobody will see me. No thanks."

"This is an opportunity, Marbury."

"Really? It sounds more like a death sentence."

"Well, you can't stay here."

"I'm not leaving these people. They want me. I'm their priest."

I couldn't argue with him on that point. Everyone that I talked to seemed to like Marbury. He sparked something within this congregation that had been missing for years, a feeling of independence. The coffers jingled with cash, thanks to record attendance. Not just from the voice and hearing impaired but from others as well. Some were physically challenged, or mentally, others were just searching for a different kind of church, which Marbury provided. Perhaps too different.

I said, "At least give it some thought."

But he just shook his head, defiantly.

"Then it's all over, Jim."

I dug into my cake, which was too sweet. Marbury didn't say anything, instead eating or just glancing out the window. He looked like a man abandoned in thought but probably not in what I wanted him to ponder, a life where he didn't have to bring attention to himself by not talking. I no longer believed that Marbury wished himself mute, despite what the doctors said, but rather that something deep within himself had finally surfaced, something too horrible to imagine, like killing a man. And yet, I knew that Marbury was capable of anything, including concocting a story just for my benefit, so I began to ask him some questions. Everything that came to my mind about that day.

Marbury listened to my concerns, crafted as carefully as possible without calling him outright a fraud or a liar. But he took it that way.

"You don't believe me?"

"It's so incredible, Marbury. How many people kill someone?"

"I did. His name was Burk. Henry Burk."

Then he reached into his wallet and pulled out a scrap of paper.

"If you're curious, I have this."

It was a newspaper article that was so old it almost crumbled in my hands as I unfolded it. The story was to the point. A man was killed in an Albany bar Saturday afternoon, apparently from a scuffle over money. Charged in the incident was James Marbury, Sr., of Albany, New York. The other man, Henry Burk of Queens, New York, an unemployed truck driver with a criminal record, died on the way to the hospital at 3:19 P.M. No other details were provided.

"Where did you get this?"

Marbury shrugged. "I've been keeping it. But it's yours now."

He slipped the article in with my notes, fully aware that I would check it out, verify every fact for myself. But that he gave it to me meant something. That the story had to be real.

He said, "I'm done with that score anyway."

"I can't believe you've kept this to yourself. You never told anyone?"

"Who would I tell?"

I was going to say that he could have told me but I didn't.

I said, "Your priest."

"I am a priest. At least for the time being. Remember?"

"No, I meant before."

He shook his head.

"You could have told the Bishop, Marbury. Got it off your chest."

"You mean, I could have told you. It's the same thing."

"I would have listened."

"Like now? Or like what you've trusted me with over the years?"

"What are you talking about?"

Marbury peered at me with cold eyes.

He said, "Don't take me for an idiot. I'm talking about Sandy."

My sister.

"Your mother told me everything."

Maybe I blinked or even tried to swallow a protest.

I said, "She wouldn't tell you. She never talked about it."

"Then how do I know?"

Marbury touched my arm, trying to connect.

He said, "Let it go, Peter. She's gone."

I was stunned. Like the force of a brick in my face, those words.

"And nothing will change that. Not even you denying it."

Denial.

The last time that I thought about my sister, really thought about her, as in missing her, thinking about her life and what she would have done with it, was several months ago. On her birthday. I give myself that now, feeling it appropriate to honor people on days of their birth. And not the other time.

"I haven't thought about Sandra in years," I said.

Marbury gave me a look as though I were transparent.

"Not that way at least."

"You don't blame yourself?"

"It just happened, Marbury."

"A hell of a thing to happen."

The year was 1959. Autumn. I was ten years old, self-absorbed and stupid, but old enough to have known better. Someone in school told me about laying coins on the railroad tracks. When a train passed over them the coins were left a mashed pulp. It seemed fun at the time, me trying to replicate that look. But in retrospect, I pray that I hadn't.

"I don't remember much about it. Time does that, I guess."

"You remember. You remember so much that you forgot."

Marbury was right. That day was like a computer screen with the letters burned into it. But ghost letters, not the real thing. Just

❦

like my memory. I replayed that day so many times in my head that I no longer could distinguish what really happened from what I just thought happened. Finally, nothing happened at all.

"I don't blame anyone, if that's what you mean."

Marbury looked surprised. "No one? Not even God?"

"Not even God," I said.

"Then you're a stronger man than I."

Marbury pushed his plate to the center of the table, empty. Crumbs were everywhere but no cake. Finished. He wet a finger and picked up every little morsel he could find, even moving closer to the crumbs that fell from my own plate. That close. Too close perhaps, for I still had a piece left.

I toyed with the idea of giving Marbury half but I didn't. I just ate instead, watching him look at me like a starving puppy. He was still the sugar junkie. In seminary, I remember Marbury smuggling in pound-sized Hershey bars and eating them, much to the consternation of our superiors, who felt that we should gauge our passions or at least not embrace them with such lust. But that wasn't Marbury. He was hungry and he ate, that simple.

I couldn't take it anymore and gave in. He knew that I would. I pushed the cake to his side, mumbling something about a diet or some such nonsense, and Marbury took it. Seconds later he was picking at those crumbs as well.

"What did you do in Altoona? No food, no candy."

He smiled. "I got pretty hungry."

"Do you remember any of it?"

"Not much. I was walking mostly, trying to think."

"What about?"

"Actually I was thinking about Jacob Barris. He expected everything from God. Maybe he expected too much."

Marbury went on to the story in Pennsylvania.

❦

He said that one of the nurses from the hospital came in from the outside with a yardstick in her hand. Her finger was well over the two-foot mark and it was still coming down. Somebody said that they heard from the radio predictions of another foot of snow and high winds too, which just sent morale lower. People were getting tired and Marbury said that both the nurses and the doctors slept when they could, picking up a few hours here and there before going back on rounds. The never-ending rounds. For the hospital was so short staffed that many procedures were canceled for lack of qualified surgeons, and even those qualified hesitated to operate unless it was an emergency. There was just no room for error.

Marbury helped where he could, which usually meant delivering meals or helping out with snow removal, especially on the roof. There was a growing concern, voiced first by an engineer waiting for back surgery and confirmed later by a lone maintenance man, that the roof wouldn't be able to take much more. The building was old and already certain structural defects were obvious. Cracks ran down the walls from years of settling. And the asphalt shingles, almost creaking and broken in some places, had begun to allow in water. Bedpans were set up. Mops pulled out. But nothing helped.

"Someone had to shovel it so I volunteered."

"You actually climbed up there?"

Marbury nodded. It was dangerous work. First he had to find a ladder that reached. Then he had to carefully negotiate, a shovel strapped on his back as he climbed, two stories up to an icy and snowy landing. The roof was on a perch above that, maybe five feet, a climb without a ladder. He packed down a lump of snow and climbed atop it, careful not to look below, for he was afraid of heights. Then with one foot up he made it.

The job of snow removal was slow and laborious but he worked at it. Marbury said that he was nearly done with half of the roof when he heard a woman's voice calling out to him from below. It was Abigail.

"Father, you better get down here. It's Helen Barris."

Marbury made it down faster than he went up and scrambled to the scene. A doctor was leaving Helen's room when Marbury got there. He looked spent, exhausted.

The doctor said, "I'm just trying to make her comfortable."

"Is there anything I can do?"

"You can keep that jerk away from me."

Marbury saw Barris pacing like a caged animal. He looked angry. Helen was almost devoid of color now and the machines that registered her heartbeat barely made a sound, only one that was slow. She was dying.

Marbury did what he could.

"Don't do that," said Barris. "No praying. Anything but that."

"I don't think she's going to make it."

"She'll make it. My Helen is strong."

"She might not."

Barris looked away. His face began to shrink.

"You have to start thinking about the child. She needs a home, Jacob."

"She already has a home."

"I'm talking about someplace safe."

"What are you saying, padre?"

"I talked to Lucy. She told me everything."

"Everything?" He laughed. "Nobody knows everything."

"I do. I know what you did to her."

Barris suddenly looked worried.

He said, "You can't blame that all on me, padre. I told Helen that she shouldn't be driving, not in this weather. Sure, we had a fight, but I ain't no guy to throw his wife out in the snow."

"I'm talking about Lucy. Her broken bones and falls."

"I thought—?"

Marbury said that he wondered why Lucy and Helen were out driving that night. But now it began to make sense. They were

❦

driving not because they wanted to but because they had to. They were escaping Barris.

"You forced them out in that weather?"

"They left. I tried to stop them, but you don't know my wife."

"Where on earth were they going?"

Barris just shrugged.

He said, "It should have been me. I should be in that bed."

Marbury wasn't comforting. He didn't say anything at all. The silence in the room was incriminating enough.

Finally Barris said, "Her falls? Is that what Lucy told you?"

"Yes."

"Then you're worse than these fool doctors."

"Your daughter had broken bones, contusions. It's on record."

"Don't point fingers at me."

"How do you explain it, Jacob?"

"I can't. The kid's queer, like I said. I cut my hand once and she healed it. I'm not asking you to buy it, I'm not sure I do myself."

Marbury said that he was about to say something, argue his point, when one of the machines that was hooked up to Helen just went flat. She quit breathing. Barris turned around, panicked.

"I'll get a doctor," said Marbury.

"Forget it. It's over."

But Marbury was about to get a doctor anyway. Then he heard a voice at the door. It was Lucy. She was standing in her hospital gown and slippers, as though someone had already called her.

She said, "Don't be sad."

Barris wasn't surprised to see her. In fact, he almost expected it.

"Look at her. That's dying, kid. She's dead."

"Just a boo-boo, Jacob. Don't cry."

But it was too late. He slumped in the nearest chair, distraught.

"I don't cry. I'm a big girl."

"Get her out of here, will you?"

"Big girls don't cry at boo-boos. They hurt, then all gone."

"Did you tell her that?" asked Marbury. "Before or after you hit her?"

"I don't beat children, padre."

"You never told her to say that she fell?"

But the question was never answered. For a strange thing happened. What was quiet didn't remain so. The machine that controlled Helen's lungs began to pick up again and with it, a faint heartbeat. The heartbeat got stronger and stronger, filling up the room from the sound of the monitor. And when Marbury and Barris looked to see what was happening, they saw Lucy there, softly stroking the face of her mother.

Helen was alive.

I interrupted Marbury at this point:

"You're telling me that she got better?"

He nodded.

"Well, maybe it was the drugs."

"Possibly."

"But you're not suggesting—?"

"I don't know what to think, I've already told you that. And neither did Barris. Except that she was breathing again."

"It sounds like a coincidence."

Marbury smiled. "Then God was full of them."

Our waitress came by and took our plates. She also grabbed the coffee, which we were finished with, and she reached over the table to get my cup. I pushed it closer so she wouldn't have to bend over but she did anyway. Her breasts sagged near my face, a line of cleavage peeking through her open blouse. I could smell the woman's perfume, mixed with the acrid scent of her sweat clinging to her work clothes, and I tried to avert my eyes. But I couldn't. I didn't want to.

I took the bill along with a toothy smile.

She said, "Enjoy your weekend, Father."

The man with the red beard, who had been ignoring me all this time, looked over right when the waitress gave me this harmless smile. In turn he gave me a similar one, wagging his hands as though they were lighted coals. A compliment for still being a man, maybe, though I didn't take it as one.

All I could think about was a priest that I counseled once. I'll call him Father Smith to protect his identity, although his identity should need no protection. Smith was a young priest, barely thirty years old when he found himself, unwittingly, at the bottom of a love triangle. Photographs were taken of Father Smith and the girl in question, innocent pictures of the two eating lunch, laughing, sharing a conversation, which were then turned into ugly innuendoes, notes, incriminating letters laced with perfume and lipstick, even erotic poems. He claimed himself innocent of such affections, at least his half, that were bestowed on him by this college girl, who, according to Smith, created a fantasy world to trap her boyfriend or just to make him jealous. Which it did. The boyfriend barged into a Saint Cloud service one Sunday, right in the middle of the homily, yelling and screaming at the alleged hypocrite in the pulpit, Father Smith. The boy was restrained but not before destroying a young priest's reputation. For there was another side of this. Late-night Bible studies in private, the odd invitation for a walk along the river, even the lunches. Perception, especially for a priest, was stronger than any possible reality. And I never forgot that.

Marbury watched me look around the diner.

He said, "Relax. Nobody saw you looking at her tits."

"I wasn't looking."

"Come on, you were fixated."

Not a word I would use and I told him that.

"Inquisitive then."

But I just shook my head and used his old line. "I haven't been inquisitive in years."

I paid the check, careful not to hide the receipt from Marbury, who expected a free meal anyway. He didn't thank me. He didn't even acknowledge that I paid but instead just walked out ahead of me. The afternoon was cold, a bright sun shining, and we didn't talk. Marbury looked like he was in his own world, as I was in mine. I didn't think about Barris or Lucy or even about the waitress. I just thought about my sister.

Sandra was deaf. She was born deaf, according to my folks, and there was nothing to be done about it. Although I tried. I was the only one in my family who learned sign language, self-taught, I might add, from a book that I had to order special from San Francisco. We were close, Sandra and I, separated by only a year. I was in fact closer to her than I was to my three brothers, probably because of our age difference but also because we had more in common. I was asthmatic. It was a childhood illness that faded with my adolescence, and mostly I had to stay indoors. My brothers grumbled surprisingly little, working extra on the farm so my presence wouldn't be missed. But I still felt guilty about it. They baled hay and fed the animals while I was watching our sister, something they didn't want to do anyway, although they never came right out and said it. But ultimately, it was their loss.

Sandra loved to draw and she was good at it. She would paint pictures and hang them around in her room. Little scenes. A mother and her children. A father working on an old truck. Language wasn't necessary to understand the story. It happened in front of you. I cut out cardboard boxes and built miniature sets for her drawings, which she had now pasted on wood. We had chairs and tables that I made from matchsticks, tiny sinks and couches and interiors that matched every room in our house, including the room that we were working in. Everything was very realistic. Even down to a model of a picture of me working on a model.

We communicated this way, with art. But as I perfected my sign language and Sandra began a new school, a state-run place for the hearing-impaired near Alexandria, our relationship faltered. Or maybe it was just that there wasn't enough time. Sandra began to live on campus a few years later, only coming home on weekends. And then my parents rushed to make everything seem normal, even though it wasn't. We were expected to play good roles in our family, everyone perfectly on cue. Dinners were all smiles. And when my father hopped in his truck to go to the feed store, practically a family outing, I was expected to take Sandra along for entertainment. Which I did. By the railroad tracks.

Marbury grabbed my arm, surprising me.

"Where are you going?"

I looked up. We were two blocks from his church and headed in the wrong direction. A block of brownstone apartments separated us.

"Do you want to walk some more or go in?"

The air was crisp, too crisp for early April. A thin crunch of snow was on the ground, and despite the fact that I was wearing a coat and Marbury had on nothing but a long-sleeved shirt, I was the one who was freezing. A fact that Marbury, with his thick, New York skin, seemed to enjoy.

He said, "There's heat inside. Nice and toasty."

Marbury would have kept on walking. He loved the cold. Not me.

"Let's go in," I said, giving up.

Maybe I've grown weak over the years or maybe I was never strong to begin with, I don't know. The asthma didn't help. But my brothers, all rugged boys themselves who became men, never made it an issue, not even when pulling my share of the chores. They didn't even make it an issue when we played basketball, a sport that they forced on me to strengthen up my lungs, even though my father yelled, "you'll kill him at that pace."

My brothers, they were used to him yelling.

The game was called two-on-two. I was always paired up with my older brother, Paul, who later won a medal for valor in Vietnam, though he should have been awarded another for playing with me. We shot with a hoop that old James Naismith himself, the inventor of basketball, used. An apple basket tacked up to the side of the barn. All height was a guess, but to me as a kid the basket seemed far higher than the allowable ten feet, higher than the tallest skyscraper in the world. And just as impregnable. The ball that we used was as smooth as a cue ball, regulation, but that was the only thing. For we played without a foul line, without even an out of bounds. Fouls only counted if you hit the ground or drew blood. And elbows were encouraged.

We had our own rules too. Shoot from anywhere. From tree stumps, near wooden posts, anywhere one had the nerve. As the ball just might career anywhere as well, especially long shots, which had the peculiar habit of landing in with the pigs. A whole regimen of fence climbing would then follow, negotiating the mud and slop to retrieve the ball again while trying to remain in one piece. The pigs didn't care much for basketball.

My brothers each shot like the great center George Mikan. They could hit hook shots and layups, even the long jumper. Of course they had to, being terrified of climbing in with the mud and animals, which they left to me. I couldn't hit anything, with the exception of Jonah, a sow who liked to kick the ball around with her front hoofs. I'd take a shot, miss wildly, then over the fence to battle fat Jonah for possession. Or for my life. Muddy, I would take my position again, panting and wheezing for breath, rubbing the crud from my nose as I awaited another pass from Paul, which sometimes never came.

As I grew older, my asthma fading with manhood, basketball became my favorite game. We played a lot in seminary, in the basement of an old chapel that was later converted into a gym. Marbury often joined us, replacing anyone who was in the library or studying. I loved playing against him. For one, I honored his competitive spirit. Though great, it never quite matched his skills. The truth was, he wasn't very good. And it delighted me. Marbury outmatched me everywhere else, but on the court it was a different matter.

I wasn't as strong as Marbury on the inside, my weakness there, bred as much from my muddy body as anything. My brothers kept pushing me to the outside, the distant perimeter, far enough out to keep themselves clean. But years of climbing in with the pigs exacted one thing. I could shoot, as much from dread as actual practice, and I seemed to hit about anything I threw up, which only made Marbury crow. He couldn't stand it.

"Do you still play basketball?" I asked.

Marbury held the door open for me. His church.

"Did I ever really play?"

"You ran a lot. Sometimes you sank a few."

He flipped me a thin smile. "It's just Nintendo now. Why?"

"We should play again. Get some exercise."

"I get enough exercise."

"Then get some more."

"Only if you use sign language, Peter. Bragging hurts my ears."

⚬⚬⚬

• • •

Marbury took me back to his office. He cleared out a space for me on the couch, which sagged terribly. The office was too small and cramped to do much work in, and he knew that. But space was at a premium. When the church was started some ten years ago, it was never expected to draw as many people as it did. Marbury was part of that growth as well, and he suffered. He had to do it all. From community outreach to typing up the programs, which now included a Braille version. But at least he didn't have to answer the phone. There was no phone, at least not one that rang here, and except for a taped message at the Diocese, no way at all to reach him.

Marbury probably liked that, being out of touch. He was in his own world. I watched him prop his feet up on his desk, in heavy black motorcycle boots, and wondered how he had done it these last few months. No words, no laughter. Nothing but an aching silence.

"I decorated the place myself. Some touch."

The walls were bare. No pictures. Nothing tacked up at all.

"Do you work here or at home?" I asked.

"This is home. What do you think, I sleep?"

"Well, it looks penal enough."

"Minimum security," said Marbury.

I looked at him and smiled. But something else came into my mind. Something that he said at the diner that I had to ask him about.

"When did you talk to my mother?"

"Oh, that. Probably the first time she visited. She pulled me aside."

"And she told you?"

"Everything. She said I should know."

I felt betrayed almost. My mother never talked about Sandra.

And here was Marbury, a complete stranger, at least in those days, getting an earful.

"She thought I could help, Peter."

"Help . . . how could you possibly help?"

"Get you to talk about it, I suppose."

"I didn't want to then and I still don't."

Marbury just nodded. He looked almost disappointed.

But I was worried. "You didn't tell anyone else, I hope."

"Why would I?"

"Well, you knew the place back then."

He smiled. I felt stupid worrying about what people thought about me so long ago, even in seminary. Maybe it was vain but a vanity that Marbury could understand.

He said, "People respected you. More than they did me."

I tried to protest but Marbury wouldn't hear it.

"You don't remember St. Agnes, do you?"

St. Agnes was a memory buried so long ago that it was almost like it never happened. The church, located in Des Moines, was an out-of-the-way venue with mostly an older mix of immigrants. Women sat with dark scarves over their heads, refusing to take them off. And huge bags littered the pews. Shopping bags with loaves of bread and groceries sticking out. Mass wasn't always a big priority.

"That was my first sermon. You sabotaged me."

"I didn't do anything," I said.

"Well, somebody did."

Marbury was right. His first real public sermon was at St. Agnes. A group of us drove down to Des Moines to witness it, but really we just went down for fun and games. One of my friends at the time loved to pull little pranks. He would leave rubber snakes in the pulpit or a pair of scary eyes. Harmless stuff. But somehow that day wasn't harmless. Marbury went up to preach, he might even have been halfway through with his homily when he noticed. Half of his notes were missing. Stolen.

"I had to improvise. God, I was pissed. And you laughing."

"I didn't laugh."

"You laughed."

My friendship with the person who played this little trick ended that day but Marbury didn't care. That we were ever friends at all, that I was in on it in his mind, was enough to convict me. As he was still convicting me.

"You're angry about that still."

"I was always on the outside, Peter. Even if I tried not to be."

I was about to offer up some sympathetic words when an idea crossed my mind. Marbury was still angry about that incident, perhaps angry enough to hold a grudge after all these years. He must have known that when he claimed to have lost his voice I would find out. And having the trust and confidence of the Bishop it would be I who would be called in to investigate. But why me?

I asked Marbury this but he just shrugged.

He said, "You may not believe it, but I wasn't thinking of you."

"And yet who did you expect? You put me in a bad position."

"Why?"

"We were friends. Think about it."

Marbury nodded. Then he added that he was sorry.

"I'm just saying that you knew I would be dragged into this. That our old friendship would be dragged in. I'd be compromised from the start."

"Maybe you weren't dragged."

"God, I suppose."

"Or the Bishop. You pick. Anyway you're here. So investigate."

Which is what I thought I was doing.

But Marbury shook his head. "You didn't ask me about Jill."

"Jill? Who was she?"

"My fiancée."

It was the first time that I ever heard him mention a fiancée.

Marbury said that the months following the murder in the bar were among the very worst of his life. His father was in prison, and Marbury was living a perpetual stay of execution thanks to what his father had done. But Marbury wasn't grateful. He was eighteen and angry at everything around him; it was an attitude that he took too far. For he started to get into trouble, stealing automobiles, shoplifting, even taking money from his aunt.

"I hated the world. Imagine that, me free and I wanted to destroy it."

Marbury said that he would have succeeded if not for the intervention of a judge. It was a first offense, this crime, a sweater that he lifted from a nearby department store. When he was taken to court Marbury said that he was full of the hatred that was welling up inside. But the judge sensed this, and instead of coming down hard, a fine or some probation, he suggested college classes in lieu of a criminal record.

"I wanted to tell the judge to stick it. But the wrong words came out."

"What happened?"

"I said OK."

And so Marbury found himself on the campus of Fairfield University, a Jesuit school located not far from his aunt's home in Connecticut. A whole world opened up to him there. He studied everything that he could, trying out classes by the handful. Philosophy and literature, economics and art. Marbury popped from class to class, an intellectual pinball, before settling on his love, which wasn't anything in school but a girl.

"She was an archaeology major. A subject I hated, all those bones and missing teeth, but I took it anyway."

The woman's name was Jill. She was several years older than Marbury and much more worldly, despite his sordid background. Jill had already been married and divorced, and she was struggling with going to school while she worked nights as a checkout for a local grocery store. He was drawn to her at once, although he

❦

couldn't say exactly why. Jill was attractive but not overtly so. She was thin, almost emaciated, said Marbury, as though all the fat had been sucked from her body. Marbury often saw only bones jutting out from her tight jeans, like the hips from one of those medical skeletons, all pointed and obvious. But she had a sense of humor and he liked that.

At least he believed he liked it.

Marbury explained that he began to follow Jill around but not in a pathetic or dangerous way. He just shadowed her. He took the same classes as Jill, attended the same lectures and debates. When she went to the library, he followed her. If there was a football game, Marbury went as well. Everywhere she went Marbury was there. Not in her face but more like a comforting background, eventually a background that she got used to seeing. And one day that background actually spoke to her, making a pitch for dinner, which she accepted with some reluctance.

Marbury said, "Hardly dinner. More like tacos at the commons."

"I take it she went along."

"She hated tacos but she went."

"Lucky for you," I said.

But Marbury shook his head. "Lucky for neither one of us."

Marbury grew tired with the story and began to fish around in his desk drawers. The sound of scurrying paper clips and pencils, coins sliding against wood, drawers banging open and closed. Finally he found it.

The Rolling Stones.

He plucked the cassette from its box and popped it into a tape player, adjusting the volume only one way. Louder. The sound of Mick Jagger's voice, his verbal scowl more like it, the scowl of Altamont, of protests in cities without protests before, poured out, and I felt myself back in seminary again, begging Marbury to turn down the music, which he never did.

"I see your tastes haven't evolved any," I said over the music.

"Why would they? I'm a man of my times."

He said this with such a grandiose air, even through sign language, as though mocking the famous words of some statesman or Revolutionary War hero, that I had to laugh. The one thing that I never saw Marbury as was a product of his environment, his times, as he called it. And the more that I learned about him, stories that I never knew from all those years back, the less convinced I was that he was a product of any times, much less these.

The story about Marbury's father and the fight at the bar, though disturbing, struck me as odd. It just seemed to materialize out of thin air or out of Marbury's imagination with the retelling. No emotion was attached. And yet his father was in prison, I've confirmed as much. Even this new story about Jill, Marbury's phantom fiancée, who seemed to crawl out from a past that I had no idea of, bothered me. I'd never heard her name before this. And the more that I thought about it, the less confident I was that the Marbury I remembered, at least the Marbury that I once knew, and this one were the same item. He was like the moon, the phases of which I saw from one angle and one angle only, which didn't constitute the whole but only an aspect.

"Why didn't you tell me about Jill earlier?" I asked.

"People talked about it in seminary. Where were you?"

Obviously not believing any of it. There were so many rumors about Marbury that just keeping them straight required a full-time job. And after a while I just quit listening to them.

He smiled. "I guess you should have cocked a better ear."

I thought about all the useless energy spent on talking. Rumors and gossip, but also about what we wanted to do with our lives back then. Endless conversations about how we wanted to serve the church. Our dreams. I had a secret dream at the time that I told only to Marbury. My desire to write, never realized.

"Did you think things would turn out this way?" I asked him.

"Maybe you should answer first."

"Well, I'm not Walker Percy yet."

"Words find you anyway, Peter. It's OK."

"But I'm not writing."

"So do it."

"It isn't that simple. My job—"

"What?"

"—I'm just saying it isn't like in seminary."

The sound of crunching glass.

I glanced at the address again and double-checked it against the mailbox, which was filled not with letters or old catalogs but with bits of used tinfoil. Drug paraphernalia.

The door opened as I pushed it, broken at the lock, and I followed a skinny staircase up to an apartment above. I thought about Marbury, working on his sermon that afternoon, and wished that he were here with me. That anyone was with me. But I was alone. I heard someone scurry to the door like a scared mouse. Except that it wasn't a mouse, just a woman in orange flip-flops.

I said, "I'm looking for Tricky."

She gave me the once-over and grinned. Several of her teeth were missing and those that were left looked ready to join the others.

The door went ajar.

I saw a man sitting in a chair watching TV. The channel was mostly black-and-white static but he didn't seem to care. He was massaging a beer with his fingers, oblivious that nothing was in front of him.

"Never heard of him," she said.

❧

"I'm here from St. Francis. Nathan Stone sent me."

The man stood up but he didn't see me. He looked like he had been drinking all afternoon. His hair was unkempt and dirty, with a thin mat circling a bald spot. Grease and ketchup stains marked his shirt. And he walked around in his stockings, which were sliding off his feet. The place smelled of rotting bodies, except bodies that passed as being alive.

"I don't talk to cops." Slurring words.

"He ain't the heat, baby."

"Then who are you?"

"I'm a priest."

He stopped and looked at me square on, noticing my clerical collar. The woman started to laugh as though they had an inside joke between them.

"Well, you look like a priest," he said.

I brushed off his comments and told him that I had a few questions for him, but he didn't seem to hear me. Instead he made me repeat over and over where I had come from, who sent me, and what I was looking for. When I finally mentioned Marbury's name he perked up as though he recognized it. So did the woman.

She said, "You mean the preacher."

I asked her if she knew him.

"Yeah. He gave us some money once."

"You mean, he gave me some money," he said.

"Why did Marbury give you money?"

"I was living on the streets, man."

"We were both on the streets, Tricky. Both of us. Don't forget it," the woman said.

"That's the story. We were both on the fucking streets."

I glanced around the apartment. A real dump. Tricky and his woman had only a few pieces of furniture between them and those seemed like they were taken from the garbage. In a back room I could see a mattress just lying on the floor, their bedroom. Sheets and blankets were rolled up into a ball. Next to the bed were beer bottles and half-empty glasses of liquor, and clothes piled over chairs or just dumped on the floor. Absolute squalor.

The whole scene depressed me.

I asked them, "You found this apartment then?"

Tricky laughed at my discomfort. So loud that he started coughing.

He said, "What would I find? My girl got a job, more like it."

Two arms made a pumping motion to his groin.

"She gives great head, Father. Twenty bucks."

"Tricky! He's a goddamn priest!"

"Once a man, baby, always a man. Fifteen bucks."

I declined but the price went down.

"Ten and I can't go no lower. I have expenses."

"I believe we already gave you enough," I said.

More laughter and coughing. I felt like an idiot.

"We enjoyed your charity. Ain't that right, baby?"

But the woman didn't say anything. She just hovered behind me.

"What happened to the money, Tricky?"

"Threads for an interview. What do you think? I just needed it."

"You mean you spent it."

He sniffed twice, trying to hide a wide grin. I knew what he was trying to tell me.

I said, "It wasn't meant for drugs."

But Tricky didn't care.

He said, "Hey, you're the priest. Go collect more."

GOOD FRIDAY.

I reported to the Bishop's office early the next morning. We talked about the celebration of that afternoon's Good Friday Mass and other things, until the topic landed squarely on Marbury. He listened patiently as I recounted, in varying degrees of detail, the story that Marbury had already told me. In particular, the trip to Pennsylvania up to that point and the story about Helen and Barris. But the Bishop seemed especially interested in Marbury's relationship with his father, and I showed him the newspaper article, which he read without comment.

"I'm in the process of checking it out. But it looks solid."

The Bishop nodded and played with his cigar. I noticed that he wasn't smoking and I offered him a light, but he declined. He said that he was cutting back, which I knew would only make him more irritable. And he was. I certainly didn't tell him about Tricky and his girlfriend.

The Bishop: "Did you mention the job?"

"Yes. He said that he wasn't interested."

"I'm not asking him to choose."

"Marbury seems to think that he still has a choice," I said.

"And what did you say?"

"I told him that he couldn't stay there."

"Then you explained to him our position. He knows."

"Not fully."

He peered at me from over his bifocals. I knew that he was debating about lighting his cigar, but he didn't. Instead he just twirled the cellophane wrapper through his thick hands until it slowly came off.

"You didn't tell him?"

"We've discussed other things."

"But not the money."

I didn't say anything.

"You're not stalling because you two were friends?"

I could literally feel those words. Heavy like snow chains.

"He'll have every chance to clear himself, Peter. I'm hoping that he does."

"I don't think he believes that," I said.

"Tell him to forget this business about Easter and we'll talk."

The Bishop was talking about the Easter service. The service that the landlady told me was a healing service only in disguise.

I said, "He won't. I know him."

I heard the sound of a striking match. Then another.

"What if he can really—?"

"Don't say it, Whitmore. He can't."

"But some people believe it. They have faith."

"People also believe in ghosts."

I protested, "I have reports. One woman—"

"Reports? Do you have pictures? Medical records?"

I just shook my head.

"Then what? Hearsay? Innuendo?"

He had me cornered.

"I don't know what to think, Tony."

I have felt, and still often do feel, that the Bishop and I were born at the wrong time. Our influence outside the church is limited, the Bishop knows that. We cannot control the minds of politicians and governments the way members of the clergy could only a few centuries ago. Nor can we control the production run of large presses, casually squash ideas with a rolling sweep of the hand. And despite perceptions to the contrary, we can neither mount an army of recruits to do our bidding, whatever that bidding is, nor stop the ones that are opposed to it. Yet it is assumed that we can.

That I can.

In a sense, I am much like my brothers. They toil away on the farm of my father, toiling away at an earth exhausted by pollution and pesticide. And yet, they continue to work. Plowing the land, seeding, reaping their rewards or bad luck in the future. If the skies are too wet or too dry, prices rise and people complain. They never complain when crops are plentiful, when the larder is full, but only

❧

when it's empty. My mother always said that's when you see people at their worst, when facing their darkest fears.

The Bishop struck up another match, this time igniting his cigar. I could feel the smoke wash across the room, like emotional relief and comfort, except that it stung my eyes. No comfort for me.

Through a smoke ring I heard a voice. "You have nothing, Peter. As for the rest, whether he can heal or not, you'll find that out on Sunday, won't you?"

I walked into Marbury's church later that morning and found him praying. He looked perfectly natural. His head was bowed but I couldn't see his lips moving. He was silent even deep within himself, a fact that made me more disturbed than any other. For the change, at least in his mind, was real.

I set down my briefcase and just watched him. He stayed there, kneeling for almost twenty minutes before he lost his concentration. An amazing feat, for my mind began to wander nearly from the start.

Marbury stood up. He noticed me at once.

"I missed you last night. I was ready for you but no feet."

"I was busy."

My tone of voice betrayed me.

"You didn't celebrate?"

"Not this year. I had other business."

Marbury knew that what I was talking about involved him. I could see it on his face, though he tried his best to disguise it. He started talking about Good Friday and the sermon that he had written about the two thieves, but I interrupted him.

I said, "I know all about Easter, Marbury."

He wasn't surprised.

"I know that you're planning on healing people too."

"Then you're invited. Come and see for yourself."

"Why are you doing this?"

"I'm not doing anything. It's only a prayer service."

"Well, it might be your last."

He looked at me and smiled. "One of the thieves was saved, Peter."

"And the other was damned. Which do you want to be?"

Marbury sat down in the pew, right across from me. For a moment I saw him as divided, as though he were waging some war within himself. His lips started to pucker, ever so slightly, as if a word were rising to his mouth. But then it left.

I pressed him further.

"Since when did you get interested in this? Being on the fringe?"

"Is that where I am? Nice to know that I'm somewhere, though."

"You know what I mean."

"I've always believed in prayer. Haven't you?"

"Yes. But I can't raise people from wheelchairs."

"And you think I can?" he asked.

"I think you're leading folks to believe you can, a big difference."

"How?"

"By not telling them otherwise."

"Let them judge my actions instead."

"Actions like what? Losing your voice?"

"I didn't lose it. It was taken from me; I've already told you that."

"Why? What did you do that was so horrible, Marbury?"

He just smiled. "The question is what I didn't do."

One thing that he didn't do was to actually accept his predicament. Marbury said that he kept looking for some way out, a miracle

☙

snowplow or something to come and help him, save him from the people whose lives he was slowly becoming entangled in. But no help was on the way.

And maybe none was ever coming.

Outside the hospital over two feet of snow had already fallen and more was still coming down. Everything was a gigantic sea of white. And the town of Wheelersburg, hardly more than an intersection with a streetlight and a few gas stations, resembled a series of unstirred lumps, like flour in a mixing bowl, except with chimneys and trees poking out.

Inside the hospital, Barris was still watching Helen, as he had before. Her pulse and respiration had improved considerably. The doctors were surprised of course, but attributed her improvement to their own efforts instead of some mystical intervention.

"She's not out of the woods yet," said one.

Barris nodded and touched his wife's hand. Much warmer. Her breathing was less labored, with her face again getting flush. She began to look alive. But the doctor was still negative.

He said, "I just wouldn't get too excited, that's all."

Marbury mentioned that he tried not to pay attention to the doctors either. Helen was better and that was the only thing that mattered. He picked up Lucy, who with all the excitement had fallen asleep in a chair, and he took her to bed. Her body was as limp as an old rag but she began to stir anyway.

Marbury asked her the only question that he could. Or rather the only question on his mind.

"Did you have anything to do with that?"

Lucy smiled faintly.

She said, "God did. He tried to open his box but he couldn't."

"You mean, the big yellow one? Why couldn't he?"

"God said it was stuck. Too many boo-boos, I guess."

"Oh, God said this?"

"Um-huh."

"I need to know, Lucy. What happened to Helen's boo-boo?"

Lucy showed Marbury her closed fist. It was a tiny fist for such a big boo-boo, he thought.

She said, "I have it, silly. Wants to jump out, though."

Lucy crawled beneath the sheets in her bed with what little strength she had left. She looked spent, so much so that she couldn't even cover herself up. Marbury did that for her. He said that he couldn't remember ever covering up a child, and perhaps in all his years Lucy was his very first. A sad thought.

I caught this remark and asked him about it.

He said, "No children. Seems odd now, doesn't it?"

"Children aren't part of the package, Marbury."

"I know that."

"But you don't sound very convinced."

He didn't answer. I must admit that I was thrown off somewhat. My expectation was that Marbury would have loved the temporality of this life, furnishing the building blocks for God to help him construct a better one. But he didn't. And nothing seemed to shine a brighter light on his regrets for the temporal world than children, or not having them.

"Then you should have been Lutheran," I cracked.

"Or else an atheist."

Marbury said that he covered up Lucy and wrapped the blankets high up around her throat just to keep her warm. She was chilled and almost shaking, which he attributed to the cold. A draft was blowing through her room, but he didn't know from where. Maybe it was just the wind from outside.

Lucy took the blankets and clutched them.

She said, "Jacob doesn't like me."

"He loves you, Lucy. I'm sure of that."

Marbury was lying and she knew it.

"But he's mean to me."

"I think he'll be nicer now."

But Marbury wasn't sure. Maybe Barris had always hated Lucy and would always hate her. Lucy, who came to him from out of the blue, attached to a wife that nobody wanted.

He said, "We'll make sure he's nice to you, Lucy. I promise."

"He'll forget. God says people forget."

Marbury was curious. "When does God say all this?"

"At tea. He likes tea."

"When do you have tea?"

"My dolly has tea."

"Does your dolly talk to God as well?"

"Silly. My dolly doesn't talk."

"Foolish me. I forgot."

"And she doesn't eat cookies. So don't give her any."

"I won't."

"But God loves cookies."

Marbury said, "I'm afraid I've never offered God cookies before."

"He likes chocolate chip."

"Would he have tea and cookies with me?"

"Oh, he wants to."

"When?"

"You'll know."

Abigail peeked into Lucy's room just as she was falling asleep. A blood-pressure monitor hung from her hand. It was her rounds but Marbury asked her to wait.

She said with a whisper, "I heard what happened."

"Barris told you?"

"One of the doctors. Of course they don't believe it."

Marbury shut the door behind him.

"How's she doing?" asked Abigail.

"Tired. Do you know she speaks to God? She just told me."

"What do you think?"

"I think we're all exhausted. Nobody's thinking straight."

"I didn't tell you this before. I didn't even believe it was possible, but now I don't know what to think. She's done this before, Father. Healed someone."

It happened several months back.

Abigail said that she was on the morning shift. It was a crazy day. A mine fire had brought in several men for smoke inhalation and every room was filled. Lucy, who was under observation for severe neck pains and fever, possibly even spinal meningitis, was out in the hall, awaiting a bed. But there was no room. People were coming in and out, including a young boy with leukemia. The boy was dying and every attempt to save him had failed. His family swarmed around him, just waiting for the end.

The boy, for reasons even he couldn't later understand, noticed Lucy, and despite the fact that he was dying he made an effort to talk to her. Maybe it was her own suffering that he identified with or maybe he just wanted to take his mind off of his own plight, Abigail wasn't sure. But something happened. The boy didn't die that night. In fact, he didn't die at all.

She said, "The kid went into remission. Even the doctors called it a miracle, and they don't call anything a miracle unless it slaps them in the face first."

"How do you know it was Lucy?"

"One day the kid's dying, the next the cancer is all gone. She was the only link."

"Maybe it really was a miracle."

"Yeah, a miracle named Lucy."

Marbury said that he had no explanation. But then he had no explanation for a lot of things. All the injuries, for instance.

"Where did she get these from? Barris denies even touching her."

"I don't know. But she gets a ton of them," said Abigail.

"And that doesn't bother you?"

"Of course it bothers me. But what can I do?"

"You can stop it."

• • •

I was glad to see that Marbury was coming to the same conclusion that I had before, that Barris was a monster to be stopped. But I didn't like where he was going with the other part of this story. That Lucy was not only seen as a child of God by Barris but also that she saw herself that way by purporting to speak with God. And I told him that.

"What's your opinion then?"

I thought for a moment and came up with an answer.

"Abused children sometimes have capabilities that we adults view as odd or strange. Jung often spoke about it."

"I'm up on Jung. An authority, except he never spoke with God."

"And you think that Lucy did?"

"Children may speak with God every day. We just don't see it as God."

"Or they might have imaginations like the rest of us."

"You want to think that it comes down to imagination, don't you?"

I did, and dealing with Marbury I was forced to take that stance. I remember far too many conversations from the past, weird and unusual arguments that he tried to convince me were true. Stigmata for one. He was nearly obsessed with it. Showing me pictures of real stigmatics whose hands and feet bore the wounds of Christ, or what were supposed to be wounds. For one couldn't always tell. I argued a variety of causes, from ritual mutilation on down, but Marbury seldom budged. And if I didn't buy his ideas he would try to convince me through other routes, visual or actual, which was meant to dislodge my skepticism, though it often succeeded only in raising it.

Some of this was quite humorous. Every year we had a Halloween party, which was more of an opportunity to relieve pent-up steam than actually to celebrate Halloween. Over my tenure we had several themes, including the infamous "Come as Your Favorite Saint or Heretic" party. I came as Saint Jerome, a favorite, whose acerbic pen and virulent behavior matched my own at the time. Most of us chose saints or the accepted heretic like Luther or Calvin, certainly not Marbury's choice of Nero. But that was his. Nero, with golden lyre and all. Nero, the lord of all heretics. Marbury entered, as was appropriate for Roman gods, with a slave on his arm, a woman who worked for the seminary. She was a stigmatic as well, at the party at least, her hands dripping with fake blood. At least I hoped that it was fake.

It was all good twisted fun. But the only kind of fun that Marbury could get away with. For such an act done in my uncle's day would certainly have meant curtains. Though Marbury got away with it as with most things in his life, with gestures of flair and imagination. The truth was, his act was a big hit, and even some superiors of ours, clearly the more liberal ones, enjoyed his eschatological tweaking of doom.

He grinned as I mentioned my memory of this to him.

He said, "Some costume. The poetry wasn't bad either. For Nero."

Marbury, I should mention, in keeping up with his character and for the sake of authenticity, walked around reciting the most horrific of poetry. And most of it was in Latin, the obscene passages dulled by Roman taste.

"If I pulled a stunt like that, I would have been torn apart."

"You've never been talented when it came to heresy. It takes a certain skill you've yet to develop, Peter."

I wrote down this line, a phrase that seemed to sum up his thinking.

"Is that what this is? Another talent for heresy?"

Marbury scrunched up his brow. His facial lines were soft and tan.

He said, "No, Peter. This is the real thing."

I leaned back in the pew and assembled my notes, spreading them out on the seat, which only made Marbury uncomfortable. He stood up and sat opposite me, partially just to stretch out his long legs unencumbered but also, I'm convinced of this, to see exactly what I was writing.

Our conversation about Halloween had sparked something within me, a memory from my own childhood of Halloweens long since passed, of endless bags of candy and homemade costumes. The school that I attended was right out of a postcard of the Midwest. It was an old one-roomer, with white shutters, built over a hundred years ago by Scandinavian immigrants. My teacher, a rotund woman with a heavy Norwegian accent, had to climb up the belfry every day to ring the bell, which could be heard for miles, from every grain silo and tractor to every farm table around. It was a sound that people knew. School was starting.

I studied with kids from kindergarten up to the seventh grade, when we were all bused, the older ones at least, to the big school in Saint Cloud. But it was never quite the same. Especially on days like Halloween. In the old one-room schoolhouse, the older kids helped the younger ones to construct costumes, which were usually monsters or angels made from ragged clothes and strips of glued paper, reflecting ingenuity of every kind. For Halloween brought out ingenuity. And scariness too.

We built tombstones in the front of our school and erected creepy monuments to the dead, including the necessary amount of cobwebs, spiders, and rubber bats. Scarecrows too. Some crawling out of graves, their arms exposed or dancing atop them with big grins. Every year the production got bigger, more elaborate, until it became a part of the Halloween celebration itself. People soon came from miles away just to see our school all decorated, and they paid a small admission to tour the grounds. Pumpkins had eerie glows to them, ghouls sat on haystacks, mad laughter emanated from nearby windows. And folks loved it. We sold caramel apples and popcorn. Fresh cider was given out. People played games. It was fun.

And nobody enjoyed it more than Sandra. Despite being deaf, I believed that she heard the sounds in her head and understood them. The haunting goblins, the fake screams. Everything. Certainly she smelled the dry, autumnal air, a fire crackling out its wood smoke and embers, the scent of burning pine and birch. As she must have smelled the leaves, rich and damp, which were bunched into piles where waiting ghosts and skeletons in old sheets wrestled and tumbled for fun. Candy was handed out by neighbors. Our own little trick or treat. Sandra and I walked around with our bags, she was always getting more than me. Sometimes I translated for her as people talked, an awkward conversation about weather and her living away from home, though they could seldom concentrate on which to discuss first.

The next day, the little ghouls in us spent, my family drove us down to the cemetery, where we prayed for departed souls everywhere. It was All Saints' Day. I prayed for my two grandmothers, my grandfather, for a baby that died at birth and others, though I really reserved my prayers for the candy. Death was final but sweets were another thing. It was an image about death that I carried with me my whole childhood, at least until I first tasted a real death myself.

Marbury must have noticed something, that I was off daydreaming, for he clapped his hands. The sound brought me out of it.

He said, "It's a heavy weight, the world."

I looked at him and agreed.

"What were you thinking of?"

I didn't tell him of course, but he sensed it anyway.

"You never talk about her, do you?"

"What's there to talk about?"

"You tell me."

"Is it important to you that I discuss her?"

But Marbury just smiled that damn smile with a look that cut inward like a ripsaw. I hesitated for a moment, then added, "I'm over that anyway."

"You were over that in seminary, so what's the big news."

"Then I still am."

But here he was with his clinical comb, not believing any of it.

I asked him, "Besides, if you know everything anyway, why ask?"

He answered simply, "I want to hear your side."

"You already know my mother's."

"That's different. You're not her."

I secretly wondered if Marbury had some agenda that he was hiding from me. Or perhaps he just wanted to ignite our old friendship, tarnished by the years and the lies that he told me before about his childhood, and how distant old friends usually become. But I didn't know what to say, even how to respond, and having not talked about it for so long gave the story a kind of hollow quality. As though it never happened.

And sometimes I think that it didn't.

I said, "There's not much to tell really. My father was going to the feed store and Sandra and I went along for the ride. A boring place, except for the woods and railroad tracks across the road. We were just out playing. A stupid thing, you saw it every day back then, kids running around railroad tracks, but these days it's practically unheard of. Unless you're a hobo or living in a Woody Guthrie song."

I told Marbury that trains fascinated me. My uncle, for a birthday present, once gave me a train set with real smoke coming out of the locomotive. And I loved it. I built a small model, in continuing my art work with Sandra, that had a tunnel and a miniature town with trees and buildings, even people milling about. I kept it under my bed, away from my brothers, who liked to cause train wrecks and explosions—right out of the movies they were—but I never let them. Trains were sacred to me.

"I wanted to smell the smoke. Feel the wheels for myself."

"I thought you just wanted to mash up coins. Impress your friends."

"Maybe. But that changed when I saw it."

A caboose.

Just like the one that I had, bright red, it was sitting on a siding track, unused. Maybe it was simply out of commission or awaiting a new set of cars, I didn't know. But it was an opportunity to explore that I couldn't pass up. A real caboose. The steps were more wobbly than I expected and rusty too, but I braved them anyway, walking up.

Marbury smiled. "You actually crawled around an old caboose?"

"I did more than that. I broke in."

The lock was broken anyway and the door opened with the slightest push, revealing a depressing scene. The caboose had been badly vandalized. Everything inside was destroyed and trashed in a great heap. There were knocked-over tables and chairs, smashed-up bottles of liquor, and magazines strewn and urinated upon on the floor. And food. I saw half-dented cans and tins, bits of crumbs lying about, and empty boxes of cereal. The place was a wreck.

I was about to leave when I noticed it, a kind of grand scheme to the destruction that snuck up on me. Upon closer inspection, it wasn't chaos at all in the caboose but a specific plan to resemble chaos. For instance, magazines just weren't thrown straight up, left to fall naturally, but rather, they were tossed in particular places. In piles. Some were even stacked up and left to fall over on their own. Like a library. But the biggest clue was the furniture. I looked at the pile, well over my head, and I saw it. An opening. Large enough for one body. Someone had built a fort, protected from the rest of the trash, and when I looked in, through two linking chairs, I saw a blanket and a fresh bag of chewing tobacco. Somebody was living in there.

"Who?" asked Marbury.

"I don't know."

Then I did something crazy. I crawled into the fort myself. The place was surprisingly cozy, with a rug on the floor and a good vantage to the door of the caboose that showed whoever was looking out exactly who or what was coming and going. It was a perfect hiding place. I found a few pairs of socks and a copy of *Life* magazine left over from the war. There were other things too. A watch with only the second hand running. And a radio that didn't work. But the thing that surprised me most wasn't any of the booty that was stored in there. Rather it was something that I found sitting in a cup. Hot coffee.

Somebody had just left.

Marbury was curious. "What did you do?"

"What any kid would. I got scared. Too many crazy bum stories."

• • •

❦

I pulled a Marbury and went back to my notes, leaving him wondering the way I always wondered. But I had a job to do and no amount of talking about that day would change it.

I sifted through my notes, the old comfort of paper around me. It was everywhere. Reports and accounts from sources of every kind, even those who barely knew Marbury. I had statements from his old secretary in New Ulm, from acolytes and choirboys, even statements from the neighboring businesses near the shelter. I tried to scour beneath every rock, every stone imaginable, but with a man like Marbury many stones remained wedged in the ground, sometimes for good.

The temptation was for me to take everything with a grain of salt or to believe very little of it. But that was impossible. For I had so many conflicting reports about Marbury that it was difficult to remain neutral about him. People seemed to take him to the extreme, one way or another, and I found it often difficult to draw any parallels between the two versions. Take the shelter. Father Stone saw Marbury as an incredibly gifted yet erratic man who constantly got himself into trouble with his own ego. He got others into trouble too, says Stone, and they frequently had to bail him out. For example, Marbury would often bring in as many people as he could fit despite the fire hazard involved. And if the fire inspector happened to wander by, Marbury would tell him exactly what he wanted to hear. Lies of course, which lieutenants like Stone would have to undo later or cover up.

Others, perhaps less jealous than Stone, took another view. They saw Marbury as the driving force behind every idea, hardly the egomaniac who couldn't or wouldn't compromise, especially if the ends justified the means. Without Marbury, the thinking went, the shelter wouldn't even exist, much less flourish, and that alone was the signature of his skills. One woman, Juanita Haba, a volunteer at the shelter, tells the story of a Marbury who pulled money from his own pocket just to give someone else a second chance.

She said, "In all the years that I knew Father, I never saw him once buy a new pair of shoes. Or anything new for that matter. I think he wanted to give it all away, just like Francis of Assisi."

When I related this quote to him he smiled.

"I told you, don't go making me into a saint."

"Those are her words, not mine."

"Look at me. I'm not barefoot. I must have bought something."

I glanced at Marbury's boots. They were so old that I almost thought that I recognized them. From his motorcycle days. In seminary Marbury was famous for having a wardrobe supplied almost completely from handouts and from the Goodwill. This was fine until we had some official function to attend, when I would usually step in and lend him something, a jacket and a tie, and despite his being slightly taller than I was, he would force body and sleeve to match. I felt like a department store, albeit a poorly stocked one.

When I backed up the statement by Ms. Haba, that I too remember him as someone who purchased nothing, Marbury became coy and elusive, as though he were trying to rewrite my impression of things.

"Didn't you borrow clothes from me?"

"You had rags, Marbury."

"Was it really that bad?"

"Worse."

He backpedaled some.

"Well, that was twenty years ago. My tastes now are more refined."

"Brooks Brothers? Armani? What?"

"Don't put me in the same category as Francis, that's all I'm saying."

He was so intent on downplaying all praise about his character, at least the praise that others heaped upon him, that I decided to cut straight to the chase. His enemies.

❦

"Some weren't so generous with their opinions. Nick Holland for one."

"Nick Holland? Figures you would unearth him."

"Why?"

"Worms always surface sooner or later."

"He said that he was on your board of directors until you—"

"Fired him? Is that what he told you? He quit."

"Your version. Something about lost funds."

It was perhaps little more than a coincidence when Nick Holland, a former director at Marbury's shelter, came to us a few weeks back with a story. Maybe he had heard about Marbury losing his voice and healing people in his new church or maybe he was just emboldened now that the boss was gone, I couldn't say. But the tale was a disturbing one. Cash was missing. Money that Marbury had direct control over.

When I asked Marbury about it, he just shrugged.

He said, "A bookkeeping error."

"Then there were several."

"What are you saying, Peter? Spell it out, man."

"It doesn't look good, that's all."

"So you think I'm a crook."

He gave me a piercing glance, as though it were designed to bore inside of me, mine out any remaining shred of integrity I had left. Suddenly I felt lower than the lowliest grub.

"A fraud and a crook. Confidence from the Bishop, I see."

"It's my job, Marbury."

"Better yours than mine. You can write that down."

I stopped with my notes when he said that, realizing that I was still writing. It was second nature now, like breathing.

"Do you like it, your job?"

But I didn't answer. I couldn't.

I said, "What happened, Marbury?"

"I don't know. A lot was going on that I couldn't control."

"And that was your job," I said, turning the tables back on him. He agreed with me.

"I'm curious, does Stone see me as a crook?"

"A crook, no. But I wouldn't rule out megalomania."

A big smile. I believe that Marbury enjoyed the attention that people paid him, good and bad, as though he revolved around a universe where, if a person like Marbury didn't exist, the real Jim Marbury would do his best to create one. And he worked at that impression. For everyone that he came in contact with walked away with some story, some weird anecdote that they seemed to carry on through their lives. I know I was like that.

"I've been called that before."

I said, "You've probably been called worse things."

He nodded. "Both as a priest and as a man."

I shared with Marbury a few of the insults that I've fielded in my day. Absolute strangers have nicked me with every expletive imaginable, many aimed at God, but since the Almighty wasn't available, I took the hit instead. One fellow even spat at me, sizing me up with a mouthful.

"Give me names any day. Just keep the bodily fluid to yourself."

Marbury agreed. "Spit's bad. But it's worse in prison. I know from my father. They practice."

Marbury's mention of it made me think about prison life.

Most of my images from this world came not from firsthand experiences but from television and the movies. I remember especially the old black-and-white films of actors like Edward G. Robinson and James Cagney, both of them gangsters and inmates, and I imagined that's how it really was. Life behind bars. I remember as well the images of priests in prison. Many of them were Irish, former street thugs themselves who turned over a new leaf. And yet beneath the surface there was a shadow of that former life that remained, just waiting to claw itself out. Good tension in films, though difficult in real life.

I thought about this when I asked Marbury whether he ever visited his father in prison. If he even could. He just nodded.

"Often?"

"Not at first. But more later. Once I got comfortable."

"What on earth did you talk about?"

I was making a reference to guilt. Namely, if he felt any, but I circled around it the long way.

"We talked about books mostly."

"I take it that your father was a reader."

Marbury shook his head. "He never read. But in prison books are your only windows. So you become a reader fast."

Marbury explained that his father, having hardly read anything before but the sports pages, became a voracious reader. The problem was, he didn't know where to start. He didn't know how to direct his reading. And the first few attempts were clumsy books from the prison library. He started with philosophy, thinking that since he had the time to reflect he might actually uncover something interesting and novel about his life. But the books were just too dense. So he moved on. He tried to be random, reading fiction and plays, poems as well, but these were just imaginary and he quickly lost interest. Science was boring. As for history, it was the opposite. Too real. And Marbury said that his father flirted from book to book, hardly settling on anything more than a few chapters.

"Luckily I was in college. It gave him a direction."

I knew about him and books. His mistrust of them.

"So you guided his reading?" I asked, incredulous.

"No, my teachers did."

Marbury said that his father began to read everything that was assigned to his son. Even going as far as taking notes for him and outlining the texts that would later become papers. He read the

❦

lecture notes and even helped Marbury study for exams. They were a team.

I liked the idea of a father and son exploring books together, really going to school together and I told him that.

"It was more one-sided than that," said Marbury.

For what began as a good idea quickly became something else. A disaster. It was finals week and Marbury, already pushed with the many exams and papers that he had coming due, asked his father for help. It was completely innocent and he agreed. He would write a paper. Before long Marbury said that his father was writing more and more papers, and transcribing notes as well that Marbury dropped off, in an envelope, twice a week. They quit laughing together. They quit talking, except about class work.

"I was drinking and having a good old time while my father slaved."

"How long did this go on?"

"About six months. Then he started to spit up blood."

But it really began earlier than that. Marbury said that his father smelled liquor on his breath several times and asked him about it. Marbury lied about it of course, but when he returned a few days later he noticed that his father had gotten rid of every book in his cell. Except for one.

"He gave away all of my textbooks."

"Everything?"

"The notes, half-written papers. My whole future."

Marbury said that he almost gave up with college and might have, had the prison doctor not called him a couple of days later and told him about his father's cancer. The disease had already progressed, said the doctor, and time was at a premium. At least there was not enough time to argue.

"I sucked it up after that. Wrote my own papers. I even studied."

A real achievement and I told him that.

"It wasn't my inclination. But I owed him that much."

Marbury said that he went back to visiting his father and they put everything behind them. School, the death of Marbury's mother, the lousy jobs, even the incident at the bar. Finally they began to read together again as well, taking turns and reading aloud. But this time it was the Bible.

A natural thing if you knew Marbury. For he always said, probably quoting his own father now that I think about it, that every argument, every scrap of what we call civilization and culture, could be found in the Bible. Its layers were simple but complex, like those of an onion, unraveling the stories of the human soul itself, where resided all the great poetry and drama and science anyway. The real science of men, said Marbury, was the science of not figuring out what it all meant but how to survive it with dignity.

"It was a revelation, you might say."

A slight gurgle of a laugh, ironic.

"You've never read the Scriptures before that?"

"Only with a critical eye. My mother, remember?"

The Christian Scientist. Marbury said that his father went back to the Bible with great reluctance, especially after the debacle of his wife and her illness, but one day he just started reading and he never put it back down.

"They must have touched a chord, the stories."

"I guess they touched something. Look at me."

"Did you think about becoming a priest back then?"

He shook his head. "No, that inspiration was left for Jill."

Marbury said that his relationship with Jill, which started out slowly, began to gradually pick up steam. But it really picked up after the death of his father. He found himself alone in the world. Completely alone.

"It wasn't love. But I had nowhere else to turn."

"How old were you?"

"Almost nineteen."

Jill, it turned out, was also on her own. Her parents had split up at a young age, and she had no idea where her father was, though her mother was a different matter. She was in a mental hospital, a hopeless schizophrenic. There were no sisters and brothers to fall back on, and the man that Jill had married at eighteen, when she too realized that she was alone in the world, walked out on her.

"We were quite the match," said Marbury.

Soon the two of them, Marbury and Jill, began to spend as much time together as possible. They gravitated to one another like moths to a flame, and like moths to a flame, they got closer than they wanted. Then one day, out of the blue, Jill asked Marbury to move in with her.

"What did you say?" I asked.

"Why, I said yes."

And the descent continued.

The Bishop was waiting for me in his office back at the diocesan headquarters. He was unwrapping his vestments and checking them over, picking off the lint and dust that might have collected since the last time they were used. I told Marbury that I had to leave, a disappointment for him since he had hoped that I would stay, but he understood. It was part of my job, assisting the Bishop in more official roles like saying Mass.

I was tending to my own vestments when I heard the Bishop.

He said, "I spoke with Father Stone today. He wanted to know how you were doing with that address he gave you."

I swallowed hard. "I was going to tell you, Tony."

"Well, I already know."

Tricky and his girlfriend.

"So you were waiting, I understand. How much did they get?"

"Nathan thinks five hundred. Probably more."

"Five hundred? All on drugs?"

"It's only a suspicion."

"What did the bookkeeper say?"

"Stone talked to her."

"And?"

"Nearly twelve thousand. But that's over two years." I tried to sound upbeat, as upbeat as one could about twelve thousand dollars just vanishing.

"Amortized, you mean."

The Bishop's idea of a joke, but he wasn't smiling.

He said, "So what you're saying is that there could be more."

"Yes."

"Stolen?"

"Just missing."

"But not lost, Whitmore. Your drug friends can vouch for that."

"Marbury said that he stole nothing."

"And you believe him?"

"I don't know what to believe."

"What about Holland?"

More bad news.

"Did you know that Nick Holland has a police record?"

The Bishop just shrugged that he didn't.

"He spent two years in jail," I said. "Check fraud."

"Like I said, the whole situation stinks, Whitmore. I can smell it from here."

I couldn't argue with the Bishop on that point. He was right. And now the money entrusted to the shelter was gone, whether because of poor bookkeeping or because of Marbury, or even embezzled by Nick Holland himself, I wasn't sure.

I said, "I'll talk to the bookkeeper myself."

"Then you'd better hurry. I don't want it spread around that the church lends people money for drugs."

• • •

My game plan in dealing with Marbury, if indeed I was ever forced to articulate one, was to appeal to his sense of reason first and, that failing, rely on the dedication and love of his own ministry. Marbury had been a victim of bad circumstances throughout his life. Not only with his shortened youth or the missing money but first in Pennsylvania and the snowstorm that he claimed to have been stuck in, and later when he was discovered in Altoona. The police, thinking that they had found someone matching the description of the suspect for a local robbery, took Marbury to a holding cell for several hours. There he was questioned. But Marbury couldn't defend himself. His voice was a mere whisper and the Altoona police, believing only that the individual they had in lockup was a nut or a good liar, did what they had to.

They called in a psychiatrist.

Marbury spent half the day with the doctor trying to convince him who he was, but it wasn't going very well. For one, he hadn't eaten or slept in several days, maybe more, and his memory was affected. Marbury couldn't remember where he had left his car or in what town, much less why. And police bulletins to find the vehicle, at least immediately, proved futile. To make matters worse, Marbury had lost his wallet. He was penniless and he looked that way, unshaven and dirty. He was wearing only a torn shirt and slacks. No shoes. His feet were cold but remarkably not frostbitten. He didn't look like a priest. He barely looked human.

Fortunately for Marbury he had the wisdom not to talk about his ordeal, though I suspect in reality the story probably hadn't come to him yet. He was badly dehydrated, living on only snow, and his mind wasn't working. Or maybe it was working too much, I don't know. Somehow Marbury talked the doctor into the phone call that saved his life. He had visions before that, of going off to some mental hospital, squirreled away against his will. No voice, no memory of one, clearly no alibi for the crime committed. And even the doctor thought these options were possible ones.

But when Father Stone accurately described Marbury, right down to his height and weight, even down to a tattoo that he had on his shoulder from his pool-hall days, the psychiatrist conceded. Marbury was exactly who he said that he was. Still, there was a question of his sanity. A man, even a priest, found walking around half naked wasn't normal, and that had to be addressed. But Stone thought quickly. He notified the Diocese in Pittsburgh, who interceded, and set into motion Marbury's return to Minneapolis, which happened only a few days later.

Marbury was now a free man. But only briefly. He was greeted at the airport by his staff from the mission, who only had to take one look at him to see that he was in trouble. Mental trouble. Stone thought that it was a breakdown at first, but then he realized that it was much more than that and he contacted the Bishop for help, who then contacted me.

It was later that Good Friday afternoon and Marbury and I were sitting in his office, relaxing. Or rather, he relaxed as I wrote. I told him about those first few days, what I'd uncovered about them from Father Stone and others, which seemed to interest him. For he had little recollection of anything beyond Wheelersburg.

"I remember the cops," he said.

"Well, they certainly remember you."

"What was I accused of again?"

"Robbing two convenience stores."

Marbury slowly rubbed his chin, thinking. "Armed or unarmed?"

"Does it matter?"

"I want to see how dangerous I was supposed to be."

"Armed. You were armed. Or whoever they thought you were."

But the police said that after a few hours of questioning, they gave up on Marbury as a suspect. The videotapes from one of the convenience stores, though showing a figure matching Marbury's general description, didn't confirm that he was actually the robber. They were also tiring of Marbury's responses, written on a tablet and shown to the detective in charge, who was getting sick of reading it to the others.

I said, "You lucked out again."

"You keep saying that, Peter. I wish you wouldn't."

"Why?"

"Luck has nothing to do with anything in the world."

"I suppose you believe it's more involved than that."

He nodded. "Look at a forest. Where are all the leaves? On branches. And the branches to the trunk. Trunk to roots, roots to ground, ground to sky. It's all connected."

"Through God?"

"Yes."

"I'm talking about you, Marbury. Not God. Unless you're—"

"Don't be stupid. God has spoken to me. I don't expect you to believe it, but at least show some respect."

"Now he speaks to you." I laughed.

But Marbury didn't find it humorous. "Through other people, yes."

I felt myself going in circles. Marbury was almost playing with me, playing with my expectation that he wanted to hang himself, burn his career and everything along with it.

"That's not the same," I said.

"Sure it is. Changed nonetheless."

He was right but I didn't tell him that. Other people do change us, maybe more than even God, for we can feel and see those changes for ourselves. I myself have been shaped by many in my life, by teachers and sports heroes, by my family. I've even been changed by someone like Marbury, who gave my life a direction.

I said, "Change isn't enough. If it were, the world would

be a different place, even with second chances. You know that."

"I do?"

"Take Nick Holland. You gave him a second chance. A job."

"Not back to that again."

"Why would he say it, Marbury?"

"Ask him, I don't know."

"Well, you better come up with an answer soon."

I was getting angry. Marbury was fighting every attempt for me to help him, as though he were invincible, immune to the physics of the world. Every action had an opposite reaction, except that he didn't believe that.

I said, "The Bishop has offered you a job. I'd consider it. No, I'd take it. Best case, he censures you. Worst, he censures you and feeds you to the press. Ever witness a feeding frenzy before? You will. You're on the menu."

My chest hurt and I was having difficulty breathing. I was that angry. But Marbury just smiled.

"That's your call, Peter."

"I'm trying to save you."

"The only one that can save me is God. You know that."

Suddenly I felt like I was fourteen again.

I was at Scout camp in Minnesota when it happened. My best friend was a kid named Kenner and we hung out together after school and in school as well. He liked to fish and ride motorcycles but his parents were strict, too strict to let him ride. But my brother had one, an old German bike, and Kenner would come over and ride it around our farm and we quickly became friends. Scouts cemented that bond, and the summer camp that we had to endure every year, except for the year that it finally split us apart.

We had to take a class from a scoutmaster named Laslow who taught outdoor survival skills. Mostly about making it in the woods with only a handful of matches and surviving on grubs and plants.

❀

But he also taught other skills that he considered more useful than just living in the woods. They were useful in the world. At least, he said that.

A short man with a great, thick protruding skull, Laslow was part drill sergeant, part survivalist, even before such a thing became popular. He was always talking about nuclear war for reasons that none of us, at that time at least, could discern. All that desolation. But Laslow stressed the importance of self-reliance and he did his best to make us good models of it. He made us sleep out alone in the woods at night. He made us take long hikes through dense brush and marsh with heavy packs. He made us swim and canoe long distances. And when we couldn't do it anymore, he made us start again. But his main enjoyment, as far as I remember, was his teaching the art of self-defense. Mostly he taught boxing, which he loved, pitting friend against friend, enemy against enemy, just to see what would happen. To see who would win.

Laslow would stop us in some clearing and gather the troop together in a wide circle, boys exhausted and sweaty from the day's hike, and pass out the boxing gloves. He had a whole pack full of them. Beaten things with misshapen thumbs, no padding, and ties stitched together with white shoelaces. After we were all equipped, Laslow would walk around, his bad eye squinting out the evening's prey. Usually he picked the two strongest bullies, almost starting the next war right there when they actually squared off. For Laslow knew, rightly, I believe, that part of being number one and two thugs, as with global superpowers, was that no one knew exactly who was the strongest, and they never fought, both having so much to lose. But in Laslow's world it was different. He loved to watch the boys rough it up, their budding manhood bruised, a full-fledged war would ensue with the spoils and the reputation going to the victor.

Having enjoyed that, both Kenner and I knew Laslow's tricks. When he finished with the toughs, he then zeroed in on other kids. Mostly friends. He almost always missed us, on purpose it seemed, picking on just about everyone else. Then finally, near the end of our training that summer, just when Kenner and I were convinced that we had successfully escaped, I heard my name. Then Paul Kenner's.

We were next in the ring.

Now standing in a circle of howling boys with your best friend isn't something I would wish on anyone. Especially at fourteen, but good training for real life I guess. Kenner and I tapped together our gloves, as we had no other choice, and took our places. Me on one side, Kenner on the opposite. Laslow rang a bell and we closed in, jabbing kind of halfheartedly. We danced around for a few minutes, barely punching, careful not to mix it up until I heard Laslow's voice screaming in my ear.

"What are you, girls? I said box!"

We tried to make a show of it, Kenner and I, while not actually injuring one another. But Laslow, smart old fox that he was, knew that. And he started to get more involved with his refereeing, pushing us together, even getting the other boys in the circle to cheer and goad us on. Then it happened. I was jabbing to the face when I caught Kenner hard in the eye. It wasn't on purpose, but he didn't know that.

Laslow crowed, "Come on, Kenner. Fight back."

Kenner jumped off the ground, where he had landed in all the excitement and he came after me, his fists up and flying. I had to defend myself or get killed.

"Guard up, Whitmore. I said up!"

"It is up!"

"Higher!"

Just then Kenner hit me with an uppercut, right into my stomach. I fell to one knee, thinking for a moment that I was going to throw up, but I didn't. I just got mad.

Laslow loved it, you could tell by his expression. He was grinning, his eyes cranked up wide and hungry. The other kids loved it too, for they knew what was at stake, a friendship built over the years, piece by piece.

Kenner countered my punches with a right that landed. I spun for a second yet somehow I recovered. But my dignity never did. I was incensed now, so angry that I could hardly even think. I came up like a bull at full speed. Two fast punches wobbled him, dropping his guard. Another punch drew blood from his nose. Then a last one stunned him. Kenner turned once and fell hard to the dirt, whimpering and crying like a baby.

We were never friends again after that.

I told Marbury this story partially because I felt that it was happening all over again but also because I remembered it, and I still felt bad. He listened patiently before commenting.

"Did you apologize?"

"I tried to. But Kenner was humiliated. I showed him up."

Kenner never even spoke to me after that. And the next year he was gone, transferred to another school. I changed everything with that punch and our friendship with it.

"I betrayed his trust."

"You just got into a fight, Peter. It didn't warp the guy."

"But he changed after that."

"He was probably changing before. Only you didn't see it."

Marbury was right. Kenner was beginning, even at that tender age, to rebel against his parents' authority. He started smoking cigarettes on the sly and other things too, but I just attributed that to kid stuff.

"Do you think so?" I asked.

"Sure. It happened to me."

Marbury said that he was changing in Wheelersburg but nobody could see it. He couldn't even see it, though in retrospect it was obvious.

❧

"That was my problem. Thinking I could leave there intact."

Marbury explained that the snow had finally stopped the next day, though it was hard to tell. Outside the wind howled, picking up drifts and moving them around from one place to another. He said that it looked like pictures of the desert in a storm, only colder. And he began to wonder if he would ever leave.

He kept on wondering that when the power went out.

It started with a dull buzz throughout the building. Marbury said that he could see the power lines swaying outside and he thought for an instant that he saw something else, a bright orange flicker or sudden power surge. Then only blackness. The town went dark and everything with it.

Voices rose several decibels. In the hallways, where special emergency lights were supposed to go on, only about half did. There were malfunctions everywhere, including the main generator designed to protect this from happening, and people were running around scared.

Marbury ran into Abigail.

"We lost the generator. They're working on it but—"

"What about Helen?"

"No power, no life support. We're running on prayers, Father."

Marbury went into the darkness looking for Helen's room. An emergency light was on down the hall and he made it there by following the beam, only to find Barris sitting with a match burning in his hand. His shadow flickered against the wall, long and eerie.

"What the hell's happening?"

"It's the wind. Everything's knocked out," said Marbury.

He bent down and listened to Helen. She was breathing strongly.

"I already checked her. She's a fighter."

Barris dropped the match and stomped on it with his foot. It was dark for a good moment before he lit another one.

Marbury said, "They'll fix it."

"Idiots. More like they'll kill us first. Find Lucy."

"What can she do?"

"Are you blind, padre? She can do anything. Look at my Helen."

"She's only a child, Barris."

"To you maybe. But I know better."

"What do you know?"

"She's not your ordinary kid. Hell, I'll admit it. I didn't want her. I'm too old for children and I told Helen that. But she isn't just any child, said Helen, you'll see. Damned if I didn't. Even as a baby Lucy was different. She had me running around like a pig hiding from New Year's dinner. Walked at nine months, she did. I'm seventy-two, padre. Too old to baby-sit anymore. I'm all used up."

Marbury said, "Maybe you're using her instead. Broken bones, cuts. Something isn't right here, Jacob."

"Don't blame that on me."

"I've seen her file. It's as thick as my finger."

"She gets hurt. What can I say?"

"Other people might not agree with your assessment."

"What others?"

"Child welfare. They might see a pattern."

"Damned if I don't hear a threat."

"Take it any way you want. I'll call them, Jacob."

Darkness again. But Barris sounded nervous.

He said, "I swear I don't beat kids. On the Good Book, I don't."

"Then how do you explain the injuries?" asked Marbury.

"Try the man upstairs. He's your culprit."

Barris found another match and lit it. Light flickering.

He said, "Lucy saw a kid biking once. He fell off and busted himself up real good. Hell, I can't explain it. All I know is that she gets busted up too. But the other kid gets better. I don't know why or how it works."

"You expect me to believe that?"

"Man, it's the Gospel. People get healed. Just look at my Helen."

Barris reached out and touched her at that moment, by instinct, as if to affirm Helen's life for himself. But even in the dark Marbury could feel his reaction. Agony. And then a gasp.

"Sweet Jesus!"

"What is it?" cried Marbury.

"She isn't breathing, Father. My Helen, she isn't breathing."

I left Marbury in his office working on his sermon for Easter Sunday and hopefully thinking about everything that we had talked about and more, even considering his options. Not that he had many.

My day was ending with Louise Howser, the bookkeeper at Marbury's shelter, and what she knew about the missing money. I met her over tea in her home, a comfortable old house on Summit Avenue, not far from my office. Her story was an interesting one. She married late in life to her husband, Alfred, now dead, who had long since separated himself from the family's old railroad money and struck out on his own. But he wasn't very successful. Several of his businesses had failed and the only one left, a small tax preparation service, was hanging on, in part, only from the talent of the head bookkeeper, Louise Howser. Alfred wanted to sell the business completely but Louise talked him out of it. She explained to him how the business could be even more profitable if he would expand, especially if he would provide other services that she felt clients were looking for. Financial and estate planning being only two of the examples.

Alfred thought about it and having no other means to support himself, did as Louise suggested. He opened more offices. And he advertised. From tax and accounting work to all facets of money management, including discounted brokerage services, which at that time was virtually unheard of. Eventually the two married, but not before a small chain was built, which Alfred sold, just two years before his death, to one of the big firms in New York who took the idea nationally.

Louise, despite not having to work, still loved to keep books, which she did on a part-time basis for the shelter. It was her way of giving something back but also keeping in touch with the one thing that she loved most in life. Numbers.

She said, "Of course I saw him with money."

"How much? If you had to estimate the amounts."

"No idea. Father always had checks with him. He was asking everyone in town for money, you know. He flashed around that nonprofit status like a sheriff his badge."

"Did you ever see him with cash?"

"He had a cash box, if that's what you're asking."

"Who reconciled it?"

"He did. It was petty cash. A few hundred here and there."

"But you had receipts?"

"We aren't IBM. Besides, if he needed something, I trusted him."

"Even after the shortage came up?" I asked.

"Well, I blamed myself mostly. My eyes aren't what they used to be. Oh dear, you're not implying—"

I just looked at her.

"—Father was one of the most honest souls I've ever met."

"But you're missing over twelve thousand dollars."

"Yes."

"And you admit that he had access to cash."

"Not twelve thousand dollars' worth."

"It all adds up, Mrs. Howser."

• • •

Later that evening.

I could see Marbury sitting in the bar even from here, from my car parked across the street. It was dark inside, a heavy, wood-paneled place, low lights except for the pink and green glow of a jukebox and a flickering television playing in the background. A basketball game was on. Marbury was sitting at a table by himself, half eating a bowl of peanuts supplied by the bar no doubt. He looked lonely.

His expression changed when I walked in. First a wave and a big smile, then he cringed as I took off my coat.

"Not your collar. Not here, Peter."

"Why not?"

"It's a bar, for God sakes."

But nobody seemed to care. The few patrons were watching the game or else staring into their drinks. Either way I was safe.

"Nobody can see me. It's too dark."

"They don't need to see you. Your vibes are enough."

And sure enough, the bartender, who before was only standing there, wiping out glasses with a cloth, walked over. I saw one of his feet drag for an instant, almost hesitate when he saw me, as though he didn't know quite what to do next. Even whether he should come over to our table.

Finally he said:

"Name your poison, Father. Mineral water, soda, I even have wine."

Scotch. Double it up, please. And save the ice.

What I wanted to order. In my mind I sounded exactly like Humphrey Bogart, except Bogie with a clerical collar. The bartender just looked at me. Maybe he blinked once or twice, thinking that I would disappear, but I didn't.

I said, "Anything diet for me. And a beer for my friend."

The bartender left shaking his head, probably the high point of his evening. But Marbury wasn't so amused.

He said, "Some mood you're in."

"We're not supposed to be happy on Good Friday."

"Since when?"

"Since I talked to Louise Howser."

I leaned back in my chair and told Marbury everything that the bookkeeper had told me, even going as far as producing a statement from her, which he read. He listened patiently while I spoke, rocking his body back and forth, a dumb grin on his face all the time.

It took a moment but he said, "Sure, I had money."

"You admit it then?"

"Well, you can't give away what you don't already have."

He stopped rocking and looked square at me.

"People needed it. It's one thing to feed and house someone, another to get them a job. Hard to get a job without a phone or when you stink. Try it."

"You gave money away for that?"

"Yes. You expected something more exotic?"

"I expected you to exercise some common sense."

"I thought I was."

"Twelve thousand dollars, Marbury."

"I don't know. I never counted."

"Well, I did."

The bartender came right by then and handed us both our drinks. I could see Marbury across from me, biting his lip. Half in humiliation, half in anger. But instead of taking a drink from his beer, as I would have, he just played with the condensation on the glass. Drawing faces. Clowns.

"I'd give away a million if it would help. Now if that's a crime—"

"It's a crime of judgment," I said.

"Whose? Yours or mine?"

"You just can't hand out money."

"I didn't. I checked people out."

"You checked them out? How?"

"I spoke with them first."

"Like how you talked with Tricky and his girlfriend?"

When he didn't respond I did.

"You remember Tricky. Quite the upstanding citizen."

"You've seen too many movies, Peter."

"Have I? Ask him that. You gave him money."

"Who?"

I told Marbury what Father Stone had related to me. A man whose street name was Tricky hung around the shelter for a few weeks and Marbury eventually helped him, especially after he told everyone that he was going straight.

"That Tricky. He just got out of prison."

"OK, I made a mistake."

"See, that's what I mean, Marbury. You're an easy mark."

"Is that what Stone told you?"

"He thought you were too kind."

And I couldn't disagree with that assessment. For I've been a recipient of that kindness myself on several occasions. I remember one Christmas in particular when he gave me his car, a risky thing because none of us were supposed to have vehicles of our own, but nobody knew. I had missed my bus. And the only way I could get back to Minnesota was by car, which Marbury supplied, that old half-running Volvo. He even filled up the gas tank for me and gave me enough money to make it back in one piece. For he knew that car. Fresh oil every hundred or so miles, and driving on ice-slickened tires only made the ride more treacherous. But I survived and I never forgot the favor.

He smiled. "Is that what you think? That I'm too kind?"

"Yes."

"Then you should talk to Jill. She might suggest otherwise."

Marbury said that he moved in with Jill right away. He didn't own very much, hardly more than the clothes on his back, so the move was an easy one. At least from that perspective. But the house that Jill lived in, a one-bedroom farmhouse right off the highway, the same house that Jill lived in with her ex-husband, looked like it was ready to fall down. Walls leaned in opposite directions. The roof was flaking off and leaky. Windows were broken. Steps crumbling. Weeds everywhere. For the first few months, Marbury said that he did little else but work and go to school. He rebuilt entire doorways by hand, replaced windows and dry rot, but nothing seemed to help. Once he finished with one project, another would present itself. If it wasn't the roof, it was the flooring. And the more that he worked, the faster the house just seemed to collapse.

The exterior of the house wasn't the only thing in need of repair. Nearly everything inside was broken as well. Only one burner on the stove worked. Lights were knocked out. The toilet ran over and flooded everything. Stairwells wobbled. Mice ran roughshod over the kitchen. But it wasn't always this way. When Jill and her husband first moved into this house, it was in good condition. Jill's husband, a real loser who spent most of his days drinking or out with his buddies, got the place on loan from a friend of his named Jack to settle on an old debt. But the only thing settled was the decay of the house. What began as flaking paint escalated into something horrible, an entire foundation that started to rot and sway beneath their feet. And the worse the relationship got, the more the house declined, like some kind of physical metaphor, until reaching its present state of disrepair.

Jill's husband, when he was living there, did nothing to stop it and actually cheered on the demise of the house by his neglect. He didn't work at all. He barely got up in the morning. Not that Jill contributed much herself. Between school and her job at the grocery store, the house came last. And when Marbury walked onto the scene he said that he felt what firemen must feel in the face of such destruction. Just tragedy.

༄

Marbury began to work day and night. The sound of sawing and hammering broke any illusion of peace. And even Jill pitched in. Measuring boards and hauling out trash. She nailed as well, joining the project like any good assistant. But Marbury needed more than assistance. It was like filling a huge sinkhole. Once he got enough dirt together, it just disappeared into the earth without hardly making a dent.

And that's when it happened.

Marbury was taking a break from the house one day when he decided to work on the husband's old car out in the garage. The car had been sitting there idle for years. Spiders had spun webs in the engine block and dust covered just about everything else. The garage was unheated, quite cold, and Marbury went in to find his coat. But Jill had thrown his coat in the wash. He went upstairs to their bedroom and searched the closet for something else to wear when he saw a box of old clothes. The ex-husband's. Marbury said that he reached in and pulled out a shirt, harmless, and the shirt didn't even fit that well. But it felt good and he walked around with it on. He even wore it to work on the car. Just like the husband must have.

And the irony struck him there. Here was Marbury, wearing the husband's clothes, working on the husband's car, screwing the husband's wife in the husband's bed. Soon he found himself doing everything the ex-husband did. Watching the same television, drinking the same beer in the same easy chair with the same baseball cap on. He started to grow a beard for reasons he couldn't explain. Maybe the ex-husband had one. Or maybe Marbury was tired of shaving, he didn't know.

"I was tired of everything. That damn house especially."

"Why didn't you just leave?"

"It's expensive to move. Besides, I didn't want to be alone. Not yet."

Marbury said that Jill, noticing his changes, started to change herself. She was no longer the sweet girl who made him breakfast in the mornings after a night of lovemaking. In fact, they never touched anymore. She started to become more distant, angrily smoking cigarettes and bathing even less frequently. Like a protest. Soon the protest became verbal. She began to complain about money and how Marbury wasn't pulling his weight, in particular with the house. By this time, he had quit most of his nightly carpentry work for beer and football, except that half of the house was still unfinished. The upstairs had no heat. Not a problem for him since he liked it cold, but Jill complained incessantly that she was freezing.

And they started to fight more as well. Screams and angry words at first, then like most things, it escalated. Once the police were called by a neighbor. Another time Marbury walked out, only to return a few hours later. Still another time Jill broke a glass over his head, sending him to the doctor for stitches. But the worst night, he said, was the night that he hit her.

"I was drunk," said Marbury. "But that's no excuse."

"What happened?"

"We were fighting like usual. I guess I lost control."

I thought I saw a tear well up from his eye but it quickly evaporated.

"Funny thing is, I couldn't leave."

"A lot of people can't leave, Marbury. So they never do."

It wasn't much of an answer but he took it anyway. We just sat quietly after that, watching the basketball game. I don't know who was playing, nor did I care. It was an escape.

The bar was thinning out. One man stood up, half drunk, and wobbled out the door. I saw a cab waiting for him outside but he couldn't get in without assistance. The man kept stumbling, his legs and arms flailing on the pavement like a washed-up bug. I thought it was because of the alcohol until I saw the bartender look my way.

He yelled, "His glasses! He forgot them!"

I stood up and took the glasses. Maybe I thought about him wandering around half blind and drunk, or maybe I just didn't want to think about Marbury's story, I don't know. I ran for it. A rubbery arm was waving the door shut and I made my best move, trying to flag him down. But I was too late. He was gone.

"He'll be back," said the bartender.

I handed over the glasses. "Is he a regular?"

"Never saw him before."

Marbury gave me a resigned kind of shrug as I returned to our table. I thought about the man waking up the next morning trying to figure out what happened. He would probably replay this night over and over in excruciating detail, depending on his memory or until the evening just blurred together. Maybe this wasn't his first bar of the night. Or maybe he was visiting from out of town. He might not even remember where he was or what he did. And that lack of a memory would haunt him. But he would say that it was just the glasses that he lost, though I knew better.

"Forget about it, Peter. You're not responsible for the world," said Marbury.

"I'm responsible for more than you know."

"Like what? I assume you're not talking about the glasses."

"Like a lot of things."

Marbury looked at me. Studied me.

"Do you mean the railroad tracks?"

I meant the railroad tracks but I just didn't know it at the time.

"You mentioned that someone was living in the caboose," he said.

"Yes. A man."

"Well, who was he?" asked Marbury.

"Maybe he was my conscience."

The railroad tracks.

In the Styrofoam cup the coffee was still warm, I could smell it.

My face was against the floor of the red caboose, hidden by a fortress of broken chairs and tabletops and blankets torn up in the air, when I heard it. The sound of someone shuffling, like feet dragging across wrought-iron metal. At first I believed it was Sandra, walking up the stairs of the caboose to get me, but the sound was too heavy. And before I could even think, debate my next move, the door opened and I saw a pair of old work boots. They had holes in them, the soles all wrapped up with silver duct tape.

It wasn't Sandra.

I froze, hoping that the person, now clearly a man, had forgotten something. He stood there for the longest time, not moving. I could see the lower half of his body shift and turn, like he was surveying the quarters, but I couldn't see his face. My chest was pounding. I could barely breathe, or when I did it was in short gasps. He started to rummage around, tossing things to the side. Then he found it. A comic book that was under another pile of debris. He bent over to get it when I saw his face turn my way. Our eyes met. A toothy smile. He was missing some teeth.

"I'm Superman," he said. "Get your own."

His face closed in on mine. And then I saw it. He had a large crease in his forehead, as though someone had hit him with a hammer or other such object but now it was just part of his face. He looked scary. Made only more scary by his nearly shaved head, and the fact that he was cutting off my escape route.

"I'm sorry, mister. I didn't swipe anything. Honest."

But the man was hardly listening to me. He sat down with his comic book, more like a tribal squat, his trousers hiked up past his bony calves, and opened it, thumbing through the pages with glee. I loved Superman myself but Superman wasn't coming. I knew that and I tried to negotiate.

I said, "I have a whole box load of comics, mister. I can drop them off if you like. You can take every one."

He didn't say anything.

"Green Lantern. Batman. I even have some Superman."

"I don't like Batman. He wears a mask."

"Then I'll pick out the Superman. If you let me go."

"No Flash. No Green Lantern."

"Just Superman."

"I like Lois Lane. She's pretty. I have her picture."

He leaned near me and showed me a picture that he pulled from his pocket. It was badly crumpled and old. A woman. I could see her face through the junk and I guessed that she was his mother.

He said, "Pretty like Lois. I taped her to my helmet. Boom boom."

I didn't know what to say so I just kept on talking.

"You're right, she looks like Lois Lane. Can I leave now?"

"You probably like the other one. The evil sister."

"No, I like Lois too."

"I taped her on my helmet, you know."

"Were you in the war, mister?"

"Bullets bounce off of Superman."

It was obvious to me by then that the man wasn't normal. Maybe he was drunk or maybe that injury to his forehead had something to do with it. I didn't know. But I was still scared and I started to turn my body in the best position for a mad dash out the door. First, I tried other tactics.

I said, "My sister is looking for me, mister. She'll call the cops."

But he didn't seem to be listening to me.

"I bet she's calling them now."

"Others taped Wonder Woman to their helmets. But they died."

"Is that a siren? You better let me go, mister."

"Lois saved me. No more camps for me."

"I'll scream."

"No Koreans. No torture."

"I scream loud, mister."

"No fighting either."

And then it hit me, even as a dense ten-year-old. Maybe this man wasn't some nutty hobo living in a caboose but a war hero. Maybe he fought in Korea, suffered injury and came back home again, but didn't know where home was so he ended up here.

"Are you a veteran, mister? The cops will go light if you are."

"I'm Superman."

"I bet they can help you."

"Superman's strong."

"But Clark Kent isn't."

Right then I heard a real sound, not one that I was lying about. I heard footsteps walking up the stairs of the caboose, the sliding of cheap saddle shoes against metal.

It was Sandra.

She opened the door and took one look at the man, at the crease in his face like a monster, and she screamed. And she kept on screaming until I couldn't hear her scream anymore.

I took the statement from Louise Howser, which was lying in front of Marbury, and folded it up into my pocket. Marbury, who had been listening to this story, just sat there. He didn't say anything. He didn't even have a comment, which was rare.

I hadn't thought about the man in the caboose for years. But it didn't feel that long ago. I could close my eyes and still see his face, the way he grinned at me with that goofy expression of his and how terrified I was. He was death. At least, that's how I have always portrayed death since then. Stupid. Not even plotting or methodical, just random foolishness.

The bartender came by with two more drinks, payment for trying to help the man with the lost glasses or maybe on account of Good Friday. He didn't say. Marbury took his beer and drank half of it in one swallow. I knew he couldn't stay quiet for long.

"You feel responsible for me, don't you?"

"It's late, Marbury. I'm tired."

"Go ahead. You can tell me."

"I'm just trying to give you a chance to clear yourself," I said.

"Why?"

"We were friends."

"It's more than that, Peter. Isn't it?"

I didn't want to tell Marbury the truth. Partially because I knew him and partially because the truth was embarrassing to me. But I said it anyway.

"I'm not sure I wanted to be a priest. Then I met you. I became one."

"Don't say I was an inspiration."

"You were."

He gave me a sheepish look, one out of self-mockery, with his head half tilted and grinning like a fool. But I knew that he was no fool.

"I wouldn't read much into it, Marbury. You're treading water."

"I've always been treading water."

"Except this time I'll have to let you drown."

Marbury didn't say anything. He turned away from me. He was beyond threats, beyond doubt of any kind. All of his faith was in God's hands and I knew that.

"You're so damn confident," I said.

"I have to be. In Wheelersburg I saw the face of God."

Marbury went back to the story, taking up where he had left off.

He said that the snow had ended in town but the wind was still howling. And the power was gone. The main generator, an oil-driven unit from the fifties, was in the basement, still in pieces as workmen scrambled to fix it. Most of the hospital was in near darkness, only made worse by night beginning to fall. A few battery-powered lights were on, thankfully, spreading out much needed light to some places, but most people were fumbling around in the dark. Doctors included, who ran from room to room with just their little penlights to guide them. It was pandemonium.

One of the doctors bolted into Helen's room and flashed his light on her face. She wasn't breathing. He started CPR, pushing air into her chest from his mouth while Marbury held the light. Seconds dragged into minutes.

Barris said, "She was fine a goddamn minute ago."

But the doctor wasn't listening. He continued working on her despite the noise from the halls. Nurses were running back and forth, thumping into gurneys and carts of supplies, then cursing. Patients were crying out, saying how dark it was. And it was dark. Barris fumbled with a match until the doctor yelled at him to put it out.

"You'll set off the sprinklers!"

"I can't see."

"Nobody can see," said the doctor between breaths. "I thought some idiot shoveled the roof."

"Somebody was up there," said Marbury.

"Well, it's leaking on the generator. Water everywhere."

Marbury just kept holding the light firm. But he said that he didn't feel that firm inside. He had a queasy feeling, knowing that the person up on that roof was him, and he never finished his business.

❦

The doctor reached for his stethoscope and listened to Helen's heart. It was beating again, but just barely. He wiped his brow and said:

"She's experiencing some cardiac arrhythmia here. I warned you about optimism. I gave her something that might help but without electricity anything else here is a luxury. I'm sorry."

"Then leave me alone," said Barris and he slumped in a chair.

Marbury said that he left Barris sitting there, in the dark with his own thoughts. The doctor couldn't do much without power, though he was trying to find a portable generator. But that wasn't easy. The hospital only had a few of these and they were scattered about, and without an intercom or elevator to link the floors, locating anything was like finding a needle in a haystack. It took a lot of hope, which nobody had.

Abigail knew this more than anyone.

She said, "I had a hard enough time just finding candles. I put them in Lucy's room in case you're wondering. Looks like a church in there but at least she can see."

"How's she doing?" asked Marbury.

"Cold. She seems cold. That room has a terrible draft."

Lucy was indeed surrounded by several candles, soft glows as from a medieval monastery. They lit up her room enough for her to sit there and color in her book, though she should have been asleep. Marbury told her this.

But she said, "Too cold to sleep. Cold everywhere."

Marbury agreed with her and tapped on the thermostat. It was already up as far as it could go. No power anyway. He took another blanket from a shelf in the closet and laid it over her. Lucy already had on three others and she was shivering. Her hand was clutching a green crayon and she diligently worked on her coloring book. One of those given out by churches and Sunday schools. Pictures of Jesus standing among sheep and with the disciples. Jesus was always handsome and smiling in those books, noted Marbury, never angry or vengeful. Not like the world that he lived in.

"Jesus is green," said Marbury, somewhat surprised.

"Green's a good color. Plants are green."

Marbury smiled. Green, the color of life. It was appropriate.

But he wasn't here for good news.

"I'm here to talk to you about your mommy," he said.

"She's dead, I know."

Marbury was stunned by the casual way that she said it. No emotion, no care at all, as though she had no idea what she was actually saying.

"She's not well, Lucy. But she's still fighting. You have to pray."

"But she's dead."

"Why do you say that?"

"God told me. This morning. He walked in and said it."

"You saw God, Lucy?"

"He was wearing a big striped hat. I guess the sun bothers God's eyes because he had on a pair of sunglasses."

Marbury was dumbfounded. He thought about the various psychology classes that he had taken in his lifetime. Ideas came back to him, theories of human behavior, the way people displace their emotions and anger on others, including an unseen God. Then he remembered that he was dealing with a child and he threw every theory that he had ever heard out the window.

He said, "This is your mother, Lucy. Do you understand me?"

"Dead, mister. Like I said."

"Aren't you sad? It's OK to be sad."

"Sad is for bye-bye. No bye-byes here, silly."

"Death sometimes is bye-bye, Lucy. For a while at least."

"I know. Mommy's playing with toys right now."

"What toys?"

"In heaven. Lots of trucks and dolls too. You'll see."

"How do you know all this, Lucy?"

"God tells me. When I close my eyes. Like this."

She closed her eyes and Marbury watched her expression change completely. No complexion. No sign of life at all, as if in a trance.

Her eyes popped back open. "Sleeping all right."

"You see things?"

"I see Jacob. Mad as a mean bee."

"He's just sad about your mother. He loves her, Lucy."

"No reason to be sad. God will open up his box."

"You've asked him to?"

"You did, silly. In the chapel."

Just then the lights went on all over the hospital. Marbury heard a loud but muffled roar from the halls. People were cheering and clapping. Marbury cheered as well.

"See?"

"I'm afraid I had nothing to do with that, Lucy."

But she just smiled as though she knew better.

Marbury said that it was about then that he heard another sound over the cheering. A loud wail. It sounded like an animal in pain, and the sound grew louder and louder until it was outside the door, which burst open with the thumping of an angry fist. It was Barris. Tears were rolling down his cheeks and his shirt was torn, as though he had grabbed it and pulled from such an agony as had never been seen or felt.

He said, "My Helen is dead."

"When?"

"Does it matter? There's your God, priest. A murderer."

Lucy just shook her head. "God doesn't kill, Jacob."

But Barris wasn't listening.

"To hell with you, brat. You could have saved her."

"She's only sleeping now. You'll see."

"She's dead, kid. But that's the way you want her, isn't it?"

He took a step toward her. Menacing.

"You can't fool me. Just by holding back, you did it, all right. Killed her. I've seen you cure other people. You could do it, kid. You just didn't want to. And now my Helen's gone."

His eyes, wet with tears, began to look larger. Almost to magnify.

He said, "I curse your birth, child."

"Jacob—"

"Out of my way, preacher. This is between me and the kid."

But Lucy wasn't afraid.

She said, "God isn't mean, Jacob."

"I did my part. I did what I was told. I did exactly what your God wanted, right down to the letter. I had promises."

"Promises come true," said Lucy.

"Like what, kid?"

"Big kisses."

"Kisses? I don't even have that now."

Barris took another step forward. His fingers curled into a fist.

"Look at me. I'm ruined, child. My heart's ruined."

Marbury grabbed him and said, "I thought you didn't hit kids, Jacob."

"I don't. But I might think about starting."

Someone broke Marbury's concentration by yelling. We both turned to the bar and saw two guys, who were on opposite sides of one another, standing up and cheering on the basketball game. The two teams were separated by only a point. It was down to the last few seconds and somebody from one of the teams was working an in-bounds pass. Everyone held their breath, at least the guys watching the television did, and all eyes followed as the pass flew up high to the perimeter. Someone grabbed the ball, took a shot, and missed. The crowd went crazy. Game over.

I saw one of the guys hand over a few bills and just shake his head. Easy money. My own experience with gambling wasn't so easy. I only made a bet once in my life, with Marbury, it turns out, wagering that I could hit twenty shots in a row from the foul line. It was a stupid bet. One bred from my own ego and probably wanting to show him up, but I won. Barely. The last shot rolled around several times before falling in. And then it fell only from the slightest push from gravity, not my skill.

Marbury looked at me.

"That glass. You're gripping it like my throat," he said.

"I was thinking about the fifty bucks I won from you."

"You mean, stole. That last shot should have rolled out."

He was right. I was lucky.

I said, "Well, the con man was finally conned. Serves you right."

He smiled. "Then how about a rematch? I'm due."

"I don't think so."

"Come on, Peter. We have a basket in the parish basement. Let me exact some vengeance on you for a change. At least allow me to recoup my fifty bucks." Then he added, "I might need it for the unemployment line."

I spent part of Saturday afternoon, the next day, in the Bishop's office. He was listening to something on the radio when I walked in, a discussion, or more like a shouting match between two men. I said hello but the Bishop just waved me off with his hand, in silence, motioning for me to sit down, which I did. He was absorbed with this conversation, smoking a cigar and rocking back and forth in his chair, his head bobbing.

I could tell that the two men on the station were participants in some sort of radio call-in program. One of them was busy arguing about the Resurrection, taking the view that it never occurred. The other one, equally passionate, was raising the argument up to another level, screaming, calling the other an agent of the devil. The rational man, or at least the one trying to sound rational, with his discussion of everything from ancient Roman discipline to the importance of the full moon and Passover, started to raise his voice as well. His ideas began to suffer. He could no longer hear himself think, I could tell that, and the more the other man shouted, the more rattled this one became, stumbling with his facts, hedging and even forgetting things. Just when I thought the two men would kill each other, right there on the radio, the Bishop had enough. He turned it off, his head shaking bitterly.

❦

"Empires crumble, Whitmore. Even spiritual ones."

He sounded tired. Burned out.

"And do you know how? They fall apart brick by brick."

"I don't think those views are representative, Tony. Look around."

"You don't?"

"People come out of the woodwork. It's been happening since the first Easter, you know that."

"Do you mean people like your friend Marbury?"

A cloud of smoke traveled across his desk and collided into me.

"How's he doing anyway?"

"I really don't know."

"He's aware of the money, I assume."

"Yes. Marbury said he gave it away. He said it wasn't stolen because that was the purpose, to help people. It's an error in judgment but—"

"He suffers from a lot of those."

I agreed.

"And I suppose he won't recant either."

"He says there's nothing to recant. Marbury makes no claims about his healing. He's smart that way, relying on others to voice it instead."

The Bishop nodded slowly. I knew what he was thinking. That he had made a mistake assigning me to Marbury. But it was too late to turn back. Everything was on my head. The investigation, the fate of Marbury, everything. I tried to assure him that I had the situation under control, but he didn't listen. Maybe it was the radio callers that bothered him or maybe he felt undermined by the whole idea of Marbury and his healing, I don't know. But he seemed oddly at peace. Almost resigned.

"You'll make a recommendation, I trust."

"Yes."

He looked at me over his bifocals.

"Oh, come now. It's not like you're Judas or anything."

"I feel like it. People connect with him. It's strange but—"

"Do you admire him?"

"I admire his strength."

"Strength we need," said the Bishop.

I nodded. Marbury's fate was in the palm of my hand and I didn't like it. I had no right to hold it there or even to wish that I could control it, and the Bishop knew that.

I said, "I don't think I'm qualified to judge him."

"You don't have to. Christ will."

And then he said, "Tell Marbury that we need his strength now more than ever. We need him to be strong for the church, strong for Christ. We need him to be strong enough to abandon what he loves one more time. Tell him. He'll understand."

The Bishop stood up and led me to the door, which he opened for me. He was about to turn away when something came to him.

He said, "Marbury has made one canonical mistake, you know."

I asked him what that was.

"Why, the presumption of God's forgiveness."

I surprised Marbury by walking into his office with my gym bag. He didn't expect me to take him up on his offer about playing basketball, with the bet or even just to shoot around with him on his court, but here I was. A smile crossed his face.

He said, "Let me see how much cash I have."

I told him to put his wallet away.

"No money. We'll play for free."

"You want to play a game?"

"Why not?"

Marbury gave me a strange look, as though I had called his bluff.

He said, "I haven't played in years."

"Then I'll go easy on you."

He showed me to his bathroom, where I proceeded to change. The bath was as cluttered as the rest of his office, with razors and green bottles of shampoo lying about, towels and piles of old magazines stacked on the floor. Most of the magazines had more pictures than text in them, crisp photographs of other countries and people so Marbury wouldn't have to waste his time reading the story. He could just see it instead, full-blown.

Marbury handed me a hanger for my shirt and pants, which I hung over the shower stall, first creasing my slacks. As I changed I couldn't help but think about what the Bishop had said about the presumption of forgiveness. It was a sin against the Holy Spirit and therefore the church, but it was more than that. It was a sin against sensibility, for nobody knew the future, especially one's place in it, and to assume oneself already forgiven was more than presumptuous. It was stupid. But here was Marbury in the prime of his stupidity, acting like every transgression in his life was already forgotten by God without necessarily making it so.

Marbury knocked on the door.

I tucked my T-shirt into my sweatpants and adjusted my expanding waistline in the mirror, looking first sideways, then straight at it, measuring the ever so slight curve of my belly or trying to imagine that it wasn't there. I might have kept on staring at myself if not for a second knock.

The door opened. Marbury reached in and grabbed the closest thing that he could find, an old sweatshirt and sneakers. He was already standing in a pair of gym shorts, ones that were too large for him or else he had lost weight, for they looked like giant balloons on his legs and that made me smile. But he wasn't laughing. Marbury was instead fumbling with the sneakers. They were badly knotted, the laces in a great clump, and only clumping worse.

I watched him struggle. Marbury struggled with everything in his life.

❦

"Do you need a knife?"

He shook his head. "It's a test of wits. Cotton versus flesh."

"You like to test wits, don't you?"

"Why do you say that?"

"Well, you test everyone at some point. You've tested me. You're still testing me. You're testing the church, the Bishop, everything you stand for. You're testing your past, probably even God."

He stopped. "I've never tested God. That's a test lost."

"Then mark one up for common sense."

Marbury struggled some more but the knot wasn't budging. I could see his face redden, the slow incline of anger, which he didn't like to show.

"Do you ever wonder about Jill?" I asked, thinking about the Bishop.

"Talk about tests. Why do you care?"

"Curious, that's all. If you're still in contact."

"No. I think she's married now, living somewhere."

"Do you believe that she's forgiven you?"

"Is forgiveness what we're talking about?"

"You're the one who hit her."

Marbury just peered at me. Then I heard a snap. He held the broken shoestring in his hand and smiled, wickedly.

He said, "Jill? It was her forgiveness that almost killed me, Peter."

Marbury said that both their lives were out of control. He was drinking more and doing less work, even in school. By this time he had adopted the ex-husband's way of dressing completely. Marbury not only wore the man's baseball caps, his shirts, he even snuggled his way into the ex-husband's pants. And Marbury got the old car started too, driving around to the local bars for a few beers while Jill worked. And this was where he made the discovery.

Marbury said that he was down to his last couple of bucks when he started to scrounge around the car for money, looking beneath the cushions and under the carpet, anywhere a few extra coins might be hidden. He was sprawled underneath the steering wheel, his hand stretched deep into the bucket seat, looking through old wrappers, pieces of hard gum and food, old coffee cups, et cetera, when he found it. A photograph. There were several men standing around in the picture, just holding up beers and mugging for the camera. It was something he might have thrown out with hardly a second glance if not for one thing.

Marbury recognized one of them.

"It was Henry Burk. The man that I killed in the bar."

"You're kidding me."

"Standing there in his full glory."

Marbury said that he brought the photograph home to Jill, who admitted the incredible truth. She knew Burk. But more than just knowing him, Jill added a devastating admission.

Henry Burk was her ex-husband.

I just smiled, taking it all in stride. When a few moments passed and I didn't say anything or even comment, Marbury clicked his fingers to lock my attention.

He said, "I'm serious."

"Come on, Marbury, I mean, the odds—"

"That's what I'm saying. How do you explain it except by design?"

"Design isn't a word I would use."

"Regardless, I went full circle. Or was sent that way by God."

Marbury continued. He said that Jill, who was now back to using her maiden name, explained that she disavowed the existence of her husband until she had to, when word came back to her that Burk was murdered in a bar. But she never found out the details because she believed in her heart that she knew the reasons for his death.

And those were because of Jack.

Jack was a friend of Burk's from prison. He was living in

Queens around the same time that Jill and Burk were living there, before the house and the crumbling foundation. Burk was working as a truck driver for a small moving company but his real job was transporting stolen goods across state lines. It involved a lot of cash and many clandestine meetings in different parks and rest areas, on the sides of country roads, and such. One night Jack went along, just for fun, but when he saw all the cash being exchanged, much of it in shoeboxes and brown paper bags, he came up with the idea of making more at the track. Their cut. It was just a loan, he said, to be paid back a few days later in triplicate. But that never happened. Jack lost everything and Burk soon found himself short of over fifty thousand dollars, much to the disappointment of the owners of the moving company who didn't like to be disappointed, or ripped off.

"They went on the run after that. Hiding out like mice."

Marbury said that six months went by, and Jill and Burk were still moving around, going from friend to friend. One night Jack surfaced again. His luck was no better but not as bad as that of Henry Burk, who had people looking for him. Nasty people with guns. Jack, feeling the slightest twinge of guilt perhaps or maybe even responsibility, offered his help. He gave them the keys to a place in Connecticut where they could hide out, at least until the coast was clear. That was over three years ago. He never came back for the keys.

I massaged the news into my brain, trying to absorb it all.

"I never told Jill about Burk. Maybe that was cruel."

"Or maybe she wouldn't have believed you. I'm not sure I do."

Marbury just shrugged.

"Wasn't she at the arraignment?"

"No."

"Then she knew nothing about his murder?"

"Nothing other than she expected it. I couldn't tell her."

"Maybe Jack could."

But Marbury just shook his head.

He said, "I'm not sure if Jack's alive. If the men found him, he's not."

"What men?"

"The men looking for the money."

It was winter, said Marbury, and he was still living with Jill. It was the coldest New England weather in years. Snow was piled up several feet high and every night the temperature plunged to zero or lower. Marbury still hadn't fixed the upstairs heat and the rooms were only slightly warmer than the outside, too cold even for Marbury. And the downstairs wasn't much better. It was cramped, with hardly enough room for a few chairs and a television, much less a bed. Though there was a kerosene space heater. Jill and Marbury took turns huddling around it at night, blankets over their head to keep from freezing, while sleeping on a carpet on the floor. The worst place, said Marbury, for Jill was developing a horrible cough and she refused to go to the doctor, relying instead on home remedies of Vicks VaporRub and shots of whiskey. She hated doctors and probably feared them too, but not nearly with as much fear as came that night.

Marbury said that he was dead asleep when he heard it. A pounding at the front door. The pounding soon became a full crash and when he sat up, Marbury saw two men looming over him. They had guns.

"Where's Jack? He has our money," one said.

A flashlight lit up Marbury's face. He was blind.

"I said he has our fucking money."

"I don't know who Jack is," said Marbury.

"We know he lives here."

"I'm the only one who lives here."

"Then where is he?"

The flashlight was still blinding him.

"Look upstairs," said the one, now sounding like the boss.

Marbury said that he heard the steps wobble as the other man went up them. He only hoped that they would hold his weight or, if they collapsed, crush him altogether.

"If he's here, you're a dead boy."

"I told you, I don't know any Jack."

The boss looked around and saw Jill, coughing her lungs out into the fold of her pillow. "Who's the skirt?"

"Just a friend." Marbury was scared.

"Sounds like your friend has TB."

More flashlight. And then a tug on the blankets.

"I hate women who sleep in sweatpants. Sexy like a bad gut ache."

"She's sick. I need to find a doctor."

The other man with a gun came back downstairs and announced that he'd found nothing. No sign of Jack at all, much to the relief of Marbury. But that didn't seem to comfort the two men. They looked around the downstairs and in the kitchen, knocking stuff over. Banging pots and pans. The sound of milk splashing on the floor and beers opening.

The flashlight again.

"What do you think?" asked the boss.

The other guy growled. "Too skinny."

"Hell, I can do skinny."

Jill started coughing again. Deep hacks from her lungs, like she really was tubercular. More flashlight.

A crunch of a beer can. It bounced off the floor.

"Let's get the fuck out of here. She's probably infectious."

And they left.

Marbury said that once the car drove off they both ran upstairs to dress. They wanted to pack up and leave as quickly as possible. And they would have if they hadn't smelled something first.

Smoke.

The one man, in his haste, had thrown the blanket on the kerosene heater. When Marbury and Jill came back downstairs they saw the room in flames. Everything was on fire. And it was moving fast, too fast for Marbury to react. The house was old and the timber half rotted and dried out, but Marbury made a vain attempt to save the place. He grabbed a bucket from the bathroom and tried to fill it, but he couldn't. The pipes were frozen. No water.

"Jill ran one way, I ran the other. That was the last time I saw her."

Marbury went back to his shoes, tying together the broken laces. I just thought about the whole story from Marbury's childhood on up to this last piece with Jill, and I could barely believe any of it. But Marbury didn't seem to care. He just seemed happy that I knew.

"You said Henry Burk had a car. What model was it?"

Marbury smiled. "A Volvo. That's the car."

He said that he drove away and never looked back. Marbury said that he was somewhere in New York State, with only about a hundred dollars in his pocket and no place to go, when he made a decision. Or rather God made one for him. He told himself that he would go anywhere the next out-of-state license that he saw on the highway was from.

"Then I noticed it. A pickup. It was from Minnesota."

"And you drove all the way here?"

Marbury nodded. He said that he drifted into Minneapolis with the gas tank nearly on empty. Eventually he got a job and went back to school as well, and then everything else that led up to this point.

He said, "Like they always say, the rest is history."

Marbury finished with his shoes and led me downstairs to the parish basement. It was largely a meeting room, with fold-up chairs and tables and a small kitchen used for serving coffee. But there was also a backboard and basketball net on the far wall, exactly where Marbury said it would be.

❦

I could see on the opposite walls behind him various pictures of Marbury with his flock. Pictures of him smiling, clowning in front of the camera, with both old people and young, some afflicted and infirm, others appearing as perfect as the day they were born. Marbury looked natural here. Something that surprised me, for I had always assumed him to be uncomfortable, certainly not in control like he was at the shelter, and yet the photographs belied such a fact. He was happy. I could see it on his face.

"I didn't know you were so photogenic," I said.

"We have a few camera buffs. What can I do but go along?"

But he didn't appear to be resisting.

He noticed that and said, "I guess I'll have to get rid of them."

"You will when you leave, yes."

Marbury gave me a kind of half smile. It didn't make him angry or upset, what I said. It just struck him as humorous, as though he knew something that I didn't. An inside joke.

But I brushed that off.

I said, "Let's play."

Marbury gave me the ball and I bounced it a few times, making my way to the basket. When I turned around I saw him standing there, no shirt, the bones from his chest sticking right out. He looked like one of those old men in pictures from New Delhi.

"You start, Marbury."

I checked him the ball and he took his first shot. He made it.

He just shrugged. "Luck."

But luck carried him on for three more shots. And I was rusty, as though I hadn't played in a hundred years. Everything that I threw up bounced right into Marbury's hands, which surprised me. He always had such poor hands. And the more that we played, the more an eerie feeling started to come over me. As though my entire view of history was being challenged right before my very eyes.

❦

Marbury didn't look nearly as bad as I remembered him, nor I as good. In fact, he was sinking shot after shot to my misses. Maybe I should have expected that. Over time we evened out, reverted to the mean. Having spent an inordinate amount of energy on my job in the last several years, something had to go, which was my interest in basketball. And yet, I always saw basketball as not unlike riding a bike. You never forget.

After a few more moments I found myself hopelessly out of shape, wheezing and puffing more than even Marbury. And the shots that I would have buried as a youngster, I found skittering off the rim for a miss. Marbury, on the other hand, though not great, was vastly improved. He dribbled better now, at least keeping the ball away from me, which he couldn't always do. And his stamina was enhanced as well, or perhaps mine had eroded, I wasn't sure. His running circles around me did nothing but anger me, and I played harder just to catch up. Two quick shots on my part evened the score. We wrestled with the lead over the next ten minutes, me running full tilt, at heart-attack speed, fueled only by my desire to show him up. Or reclaim what I always enjoyed over him on the court. Complete superiority.

Marbury broke his joined hands apart in one motion.

He said, "Water break."

"Are you tired?"

I puffed so hard that the words hardly sounded like any intelligible language, just garble. And my knees, supporting the full weight of my arms on them, wobbled with exhaustion. He was killing me.

"Just thirsty," said Marbury.

He was cool and relaxed. A faint bead of sweat crossed his brow, the only thing betraying any sense that he was exercising.

"I wanted to tell you about Pennsylvania."

"Now?"

"We can do both. Rest and talk."

Marbury paused at the water bottle, his lips pursed. He said that Barris left after telling everyone the awful news that Helen was dead. Marbury was crushed. He had invested so much into hoping that Helen would make it, and despite not knowing her or even having ever talked to her before, he said that he felt a rapport. But Lucy seemed to show no emotion at all.

"You see this sometimes with children. Abused ones especially."

"So you were finally convinced that she was abused?" I asked.

"At that point I was, yes."

Marbury said that he tried to start a dialogue with her, which was difficult because she didn't seem to understand the gravity of the situation.

He said, "She was your mother, Lucy. I'm very sorry."

"Don't be so sorry."

"Aren't you?"

"No. I still have her boo-boo."

She held up her tiny fist, which was still closed.

"I think you can let it go now. She's gone."

Marbury looked at her. A tear came to his eye just thinking about what would happen to Lucy now that Barris was so distraught. Maybe a foster home. He simply couldn't be trusted anymore with her, Marbury knew that. Broken bones could easily become something else. Something much worse and violent.

He said, "I'm afraid your mother's resting with God now, Lucy. But I'll take care of you. You won't have to go back to Jacob anymore, I promise."

"What about my dolly?"

"She can come with you."

"Dolly likes her room. Jacob made her a chair."

"I'll get the chair back."

"It rocks, you know."

"Your dolly's chair will rock in any room, Lucy."

"But it won't be my room."

"You'll have a brand-new room."

"Not with stars. I have stars over my bed. They glow."

"There are stars everywhere."

"And a moon. I want my moon."

"I'll find you a new moon."

"And God too. God likes my room."

"God follows you everywhere, Lucy."

"It's cold, mister."

"I know. It won't be cold anymore, I promise."

She fell back on her pillow and Marbury covered her up even tighter than before. Lucy was freezing.

She said, "I still have the boo-boo, mister."

"Let it go, Lucy."

"It's in my hand."

"Then give it to me," he said.

"You won't drop it."

"I'll hold on tight. I promise."

Lucy cracked a faint smile and with her eyes starting to nod off to dreamland she relaxed her fingers.

She said, "Say hello to Mommy for me."

Marbury didn't pay attention to that and just scrounged up another blanket from the closet. But she was so cold. He could feel her little body shaking, teeth chattering. Marbury opened up the door and propped it, to get some heat from the hall. But that didn't work. Like a fireplace with an open flue the room just became colder.

"Can someone get a space heater in here?"

One of the supply nurses went looking for one and came back with a few electric heating packs. She went in to hook them up.

"It's freezing in here. We'll move her next door, Father."

"Is she OK?"

"Probably a draft."

"She doesn't look well," said Marbury. "You know that she's diabetic."

"I'll take care of it."

Marbury was about to help, moving the bed and Lucy in it, when he heard something, a loud wail. It was from Barris.

Marbury excused himself and ran down the hall to find out what was going on. He half wondered to himself whether Barris had finally gone off the edge and injured himself, or worse, injured the closest doctor that he could find. But he was wrong. Barris wasn't hurt, Marbury discovered. He was just leaning against a wall—the wall holding him up, more like it—a stunned expression on his face.

"What is it?"

Barris stammered, "It's Helen—"

"I'm sorry, Jacob. I—"

"No, no. She just asked for a glass of water."

I screwed the plastic cap back on the water bottle and looked at it. Strange timing. Meanwhile, Marbury was bouncing the ball in between his legs with uncanny skill, grinning and acting like he could whistle without actually doing it. I was beginning to feel that I was being played a fool and I didn't like it one bit.

I said, "You're telling me a dead woman asked for water?"

He pulled up. "That's exactly what I'm telling you."

"How is this possible?"

"I don't know."

"Well, what did the doctors say?"

"They didn't believe it. But then none of them actually saw her dead."

"There you go. It was a setup."

"By who?"

"Barris. Surely you didn't trust him?"

"She was pulled from a wreck in front of my eyes, Peter. I saw it."

"So?"

"So she was dying. I could even see that."

"Dead people don't sit up, Marbury, except in horror movies."

He shrugged. "This one did."

But Marbury said that he understood my reluctance to believe the story. He had a tough time believing it himself at first, instead focusing on what nobody thought about. The electricity. Helen was left on the life support machines throughout the power outage, and once they came back on so presumably did the machines.

"It was an explanation. But not the real one."

"I guess you're going to say next that you healed her."

"No. Lucy did."

Marbury said that he was listening to what Helen was telling a doctor, about how she felt, following his penlight with her eyes, when Abigail pulled him to the side. Her voice was almost a whisper.

She said, "It's Lucy. I think she's in trouble."

Marbury left to find a bevy of doctors huddled in Lucy's room. They were bent over and looking at her, flashing lights into her eyes and talking in medical talk. But Lucy wasn't responding.

"What's happening?" yelled Marbury.

Abigail said, "She's unconscious. But she's in good hands."

The doctors kept mumbling to themselves but Lucy wasn't moving.

Marbury turned pale, almost white. He felt woozy, as though he would pass out, and might have had he not propped himself up, his arm bracing the back of a chair for support.

Then it came to him. She was in insulin shock.

"Did she get her insulin?"

"Insulin?" Abigail blinked.

From the back of the room a voice spoke up.

It was the supply nurse. "She's diabetic, Abby."

Abigail's face started to twist in horror. "She isn't diabetic."

"I checked her blood sugar myself."

"I'm telling you, she's isn't diabetic."

"But Father said—"

Marbury was stunned. "She wears an ID bracelet."

One of the doctors, upon hearing this, picked up the child's arm. A metal bracelet dangled in the air.

"He's right!"

But Abigail just shook her head.

"That's not her bracelet," she said. "It's her mother's. She's the diabetic."

"But surely insulin won't hurt her?" asked Marbury. "Will it?"

We continued our game but I wasn't playing well. At least as well as I once remember playing against him. Easy shots I missed. Layups and open jump shots went wild, rolling off the rim straight into Marbury's reaching arms. And the shots that he made were ones that I thought to be impossible for him, hook shots and long bombs that in seminary he'd always attempted but to no avail. Now everything that he threw up went in, making him look more invincible and me only more hapless.

I tried to make up for my lack of a game with sheer hustle and determination. I challenged every shot, I dribbled around in circles trying to tire him out, I rebounded with a fury reserved for a larger man than myself. But none of it worked. I was still falling behind. After Marbury sunk two more shots he called time, taking pity on me and my lungs before he readied me for the final doom.

"Guess I'm hot today," he said.

I wanted to wipe that smile off of his face and might have with my fist if not for something that I remembered. Once a week in seminary, I punished him just like this, whether in a game or one-on-one, I creamed Marbury like no man before was ever creamed. And I showed him little mercy. Certainly not half the grace that he was showing me. He took the beatings well, unlike myself, and I never saw him as a loser, only as a man out of his element.

"You're in good shape," I said.

But Marbury said that wasn't always the case. Before he left for Pennsylvania he was at the lowest point in his life, made only lower by the fact that he didn't know exactly how low he was.

"I was fat. Not blubber fat but fat thinking. A real hotshot, I thought I knew everything. But God shut me up."

"Or you elected to shut yourself up."

"And why would I do that?"

"I don't know. Maybe this is your idea of a joke."

"It's no joke, Peter."

"Then say something. Say something and I might be able to help you."

"What can you do?"

"I'll talk to the Bishop."

But Marbury just shook his head.

He said, "I want to speak. Lord knows I try every day."

"Do you?"

"Yes, but it's gone."

I must have given him a nasty look, for he added, "Haven't you ever lost anything before? It's horrible."

He knew that I had.

Maybe Marbury didn't mean it that way or maybe he did and I was just kidding myself. I don't know. But my thoughts went back to that day with Sandra and suddenly I was there again. I could see the whole scene unfold before my eyes.

We were at the railroad tracks.

Sandra saw the man from the caboose and took off running. I don't know how but I bolted out as well, and the man didn't try to stop me. Not at first. I was a few steps out of the caboose door and already down the stairs when I heard him yelling.

"Superman!"

But I just kept on running. Sandra was ahead of me, running at full speed. Her feet were flying along the railroad ties, taking two or three at a time. She was petrified. I ran as hard as I could, hoping that I could intercept her but I just couldn't catch up. She couldn't hear me. She didn't even know I was behind her. My chest started to burn as I ran and I began to wheeze and cough.

It was my asthma.

"You'll forget Superman!"

The man from the caboose was closing in on me. I started to run as fast as I could but I was falling behind. Sandra was ahead of me, crossing a thicket of trees right at the crossing signal. But the signal wasn't on.

I turned around to find the man almost on top of me. I tried to push it but I just collapsed; my lungs were getting the best of me. The man trotted up and looked down at me. I thought that he was going to grab me, take me back to his caboose or something horrible, but he didn't. He just smiled.

"Take Superman. I've already read it."

And he handed me his comic book.

I couldn't breathe. My heart was pounding, my head hurt. But the man just stood there. He didn't do anything.

Then I heard a whistle.

"Four o'clock. Choo-choo."

And he smiled.

Game point.

Marbury threw up a shot that missed, giving me a golden opportunity to take advantage. Thanks to my fierce play I managed to hack my way back up to even the score, a real accomplishment considering just how badly I was playing. I took the ball at the top of the key, or more likely where the key would have been if a podium wasn't there first, and made my move. I dribbled a few times and spun to my left, a move that in my heyday would have faked Marbury out of everything below his belt. But not this time. He stuck to me like damp chalk, following me to the basket as my shot soared wide. He took the rebound, stepped back, and gunned.

A winning basket.

The ball bounced on the floor until it died. I lost. In all my years of playing Marbury I had never lost; I had not even come close to losing. And he seemed to recognize the occasion, the rarity of it, for he smiled.

He said, "Easy roll. It's the rim."

Marbury was being gracious. But the truth was I knew better. He beat me, thrashed me soundly, despite the score. A part of me could blame it on my physical condition or on the fact that I was rusty. I hadn't played in several months. But that didn't cut water. I lost because I assumed myself to be better, fat, in Marbury's words, presuming to know the outcome of something before it even began. I was no better off than Marbury; I was just presuming something different.

"It's only a game, Peter. Forget about it."

I glanced at him, his blue eyes flashing delight. And then it came to me. An image of him in the pool hall, hustling all comers into a contest of wit and guile. What if Marbury had always held back, even in seminary? What if he never played as well as he could? Maybe Marbury was like one of those Zen masters who perfected failure as some bizarre form of meditation. Where would that leave me? All those years of gloating, my personal reveling in his destruction on the court, might have been nothing but a giant sham. A simple con.

"You weren't dogging me, were you, Marbury?"

"What do you mean?"

❧

"Well, this is a first. You never win."

He didn't say anything. He didn't have to. My own imagination was saying enough. Maybe Marbury was tired of my dominance over the years and practiced for this moment. Working himself with hours of dribbling and shooting just on the off chance that we might meet up again. Maybe he even planned it that way, mysteriously losing his voice just to force this game and his eventual outcome in it. Or the lost voice itself might be the real game here, the final victory to negate every other defeat in his life. His father, his mother, Jill, the man Burk in the bar. I could have kept on thinking these thoughts until I realized something. That's what a con man does. He forces you up against yourself.

I said, "I'm just surprised, that's all. I thought you didn't play."

"I don't play. Doesn't mean I still don't shoot around."

I took his explanation in stride. Whatever the reason, I'd lost.

"I guess a guy can't lose forever, Marbury."

Words that I pulled out from my past. For I'm not sure that I really believed it. Growing up, watching certain farmers lose year in and year out, despite the weather, despite the lay of the land, had taught me otherwise. My father always referred to these poor fellows as unlucky, without any hope of luck, which only made me think about the opposite of that. The lucky. That was us, for a while. Our farm prospered. Even during rough times we somehow averted disaster, whether by our wits or luck or just plain intelligence I could never quite figure out. Sometimes it was hot and people lost their corn, but we rarely did. It was the same with other crops, and even our animals. We sold at always the right time. Never low enough to bury us; never too high to make us zealous. It was like someone was looking out for us.

My mother said that someone was God. That God looked out for all pious people everywhere, helping them whenever the Almighty deemed it necessary to intervene. And I grew up with that explanation, I might even have believed it until that day when I realized that we weren't so lucky, just awaiting our turn at life's guillotine.

It started when my father got sick, several months before Sandra and the railroad tracks. He never had a good heart but we didn't think much about it, he was so strong. But a heart attack changed all that. He became frail, losing fifty or so pounds of muscle built up over the years by hoisting hay and seed. My brothers took over the farm, except that they were only kids themselves, still in school, and we needed to hire help, which was expensive. But we persevered this way for over two years, everyone pitching in where they could.

At least until the grasshoppers came.

It was the hottest summer on record, I remember that. No rain for two months straight. And the only clouds were clouds of grasshoppers moving across the fields like hungry demons. You couldn't walk without crushing a fistful of them. They would jump through crops and strip a field bare. What there was left to strip. For the ground was like concrete, hard and cracked like those pictures of the desert in magazines. Except that this desert was our own land. Entire lakes dried up under the scorching heat. Rivers ran into nowhere. Fish died. Leaves turned brown well before autumn. And the heat made everything brittle, ready for a match, lives as well.

We went into debt that summer. My father sold a tractor just to make ends meet. But that didn't last long. He had a payroll to meet and when he couldn't pay anymore the workers just left. No sympathy, for they had families to feed as well. We sent more animals to slaughter but prices were low, and the luck that we enjoyed all those years expired without so much as a friendly good-bye.

A man can't lose forever. My father said that, walking around with a cane, his crops dying, the grasshoppers eating up the last of his self-respect. He said it as a rallying point for the family, but I don't think he saw it that way. For we were surrounded by losers. People who had lost farms, fathers who had lost sons in wars, mothers who had lost daughters, people who had lost faith. In life, it sometimes seemed that people could go on losing forever and often did, though they called it something else.

Marbury gave me a sideways glance.

He said, "Losing I've never been afraid of. It tempers one anyway."

I've heard people say that before. On radio, on television talk shows, in self-help books. But I must admit to never believing any of it. Nobody likes pain, and even if that pain could be exchanged for something else, something greater than the sum of its parts, it could never equal the pain itself.

"I don't believe that, Marbury. Steel is tempered but it's hard. It's hard because it can't feel. Same with people. Push them hard enough and they wind up feeling nothing. They wind up as nothing."

I was breathing fast, almost blurting out my words.

"Is that what happened to you, Peter?"

I just looked at him.

"Your mother said you witnessed it."

"I saw everything, yes."

"Even the train?"

The train.

I could hear the whistle but I was wheezing too bad to move. My sister was still running and she never turned around. The man from the caboose was just standing there making sounds with the whistle, going choo-choo like he was a little kid.

And then it turned a corner.

I looked up and saw the brakeman. But he couldn't see what it was that I was seeing, Sandra going at a direct intercept. She was running past the few inactive tracks down a small ravine and then up again where the main track was. Trees were on one side. Another blast from the whistle.

She couldn't hear it.

The man from the caboose stopped his idiotic whistling and started running. He didn't know that Sandra was deaf but he could see what was happening. I never saw anyone sprint so fast. He was like some sort of wild animal, jumping over holes and logs trying to get to her. Then I started running as well, I had to, but my lungs were failing me.

The train took the last stretch and the brakeman blew the whistle. His view was still blocked by the trees and he slowed down just a bit. Not nearly slow enough. Sandra turned now, the only time she ever did, and saw the man from the caboose running after her. She only ran faster.

The caboose man was closing in and I was right behind, puffing along. But the train was faster. Sandra made a last dash across the trees. I knew where she was going. Across the road to my father, who was probably finishing his business at the feed store.

But she never made it.

Everything went into a dream after that. I saw a body flying and the sound of screeching metal brakes. Sparks and fire and smoke filled the air. The man from the caboose, thinking that he was at war again perhaps or maybe aghast with the horror, threw his arms over his face and screamed. I screamed too.

The train limped to a stop a few hundred yards later. Several men ran out of the locomotive yelling and acting all frantic. I caught up to the man from the caboose by now, who was standing over Sandra's body. One of the men pushed him out of the way and slid into her, tearing open a medical kit. But he didn't need one.

"Aw, Christ! No! No!" he said.

Voices and confusion.

"I didn't see her!" cried the brakeman.

"Nobody saw her."

"But the whistle—?"

"To hell with the whistle!"

Another one said, "I'll radio a doctor."

But the first guy just grabbed his arm.

He said, "Radio an undertaker. She's dead."

"What should I say?"

"Tell them it's an accident."

Double take on the man from the caboose.

"—tell them we're not sure."

My house after Sandra's death wasn't like a real place. Or maybe it was too real. Nobody talked about it even though we all walked around like zombies. At night I could hear my mother downstairs at the kitchen table, praying, her words low and mumbled as though she was too embarrassed to voice them aloud. But I knew what she was doing anyway. At least she knew that Sandra was dead. More than my father, who just blocked her out of his mind. He never prayed again. And he never stepped back into a church again after the funeral. He was done with God, I knew that.

Gradually, and this is the incredible thing, gradually life began to come back. Baths were taken again, food eaten, cars driven. We went on. But our luck was never the same. Sandra's name was never mentioned again in our house. Her photographs were stripped from the walls, along with the needlework and paintings that she gave to my parents. And the contents of her room were packed up. Sold off. Clothes were donated to the Goodwill. Gone were her dolls, her bike, her bed, and all her furniture. Gone too were her memories, for it was like she had never existed, or just walked away one day and vanished. Even in our minds.

I tried to join the family in their denial but I wasn't always as successful. Sandra would just pop into my mind for no apparent explanation. I certainly wasn't thinking about her. I avoided that like everyone else, but there she would be. Not that I could talk about it. Nobody wanted to hear anything that I had to say. Even after the accident I never had the opportunity to explain myself, to tell people what I really saw. My mother didn't ask me what happened, having learned it from my father, and he didn't try to clarify anything. He just went along with my story.

I remember once, months after the incident, that I tried to tell my teacher. It was after school and I waited for everyone to leave, thinking that I would get a sympathetic ear. But instead I got someone who didn't know what to say, and not knowing, she just tried to say everything. I could barely spit a word out edgewise. My teacher talked about God and how everything had a purpose, even things so horrible that we can't imagine them, and then she started quoting things, people that I've never heard of, until she lost steam and I lost the desire to say anything else.

I haven't opened my mouth about the incident since.

Marbury looked at me and said that he was sorry. But I just shrugged him off. Sorry counted three decades ago, not now.

"You have to worry about yourself, Marbury."

"What's the worst on my plate?"

"A tribunal," I said.

"Oh, it won't come to that. Trust me."

"Then you agree to my conditions? First, a declaration that you can't heal, could never heal, and a disavowal of everyone who claims to have been healed by you."

"Don't forget about my desk job."

"That's already waiting for you."

Marbury smiled and twirled the ball on his index finger like a pro. It fell off only when it quit spinning.

He said, "I have a better idea. Let's shoot for it, Peter. First one to miss caves in. What do you say?"

I said that I couldn't.

"Too bad. Then I guess I'll have to wait for the cavalry."

I left Marbury after that. I was sweaty and tired and every vein in my head throbbed and ached. At home I ran a bath and sat in it, nursing a few bottles of beer and thinking, but the dirt just wouldn't soak off me.

The sun must have woke me up, for my eyes opened. A streamer of light ran from my outside window down to the tub, where I had fallen asleep, and it hit me in the face. Warmth.

It was Easter Sunday.

I got to Marbury's office a few hours before Mass. He was sitting there, his feet propped up on his desk reading a newspaper. Not a care in the world. He took one look at me and smiled.

"Your skin. Are those wrinkles on your hands?"

I looked down. White prunes attached to my wrists.

"You're not suddenly aging on me, are you?"

"Just a long shower."

"You still take long showers?" He smiled.

I brushed him off by pushing a pile of books from the couch, which mysteriously had gotten there overnight like a growing fungus, and onto the floor. A loud crash. But Marbury didn't flinch from his article. He was used to chaos.

The sun was beaming through his window as well. It was cold outside, maybe forty degrees, but the sky was the color of the sea,

ᢙᡢᢩ

a washing of blue. And it felt like Easter. I thought about all the Easters in my life, a kind of rapid montage of places and events and people too. Then it came to me.

"What are you laughing about?" asked Marbury.

"I was thinking about seminary. The guy with the cross."

"Sure, you mean Lou Waters."

"God, you actually know his name?"

"Why not?"

The man that I was referring to was seen only once a year. On Easter. Whether he was a local or a vagrant who just drifted in for the occasion, I don't know. But I was shocked that Marbury actually knew him, for everyone saw him as a nut. He always showed up on the chapel stairs around sunrise, thinking that he was the resurrected Christ, I suppose, wearing only a cloak and sandals. He wore a crown of thorns as well but nobody noticed that. They only noticed the cross.

It was huge. Maybe eight feet long made from real lumber that was hammered together. He dragged that damn cross around every year on Easter morning, signifying exactly what I had no idea, for it wasn't Good Friday. And he never said anything. Not a sermon. Not even a quote from Revelation, which was usually standard fare.

"You spoke to him?" I asked.

"I took him to lunch. Of course, he had to park the cross."

I almost burst out laughing. The thought of Marbury feeding the Jesus man, as he was later to be known, was the craziest thing that I've ever heard. I could imagine them together at a diner, everyone in town glancing up from their soup and cheeseburgers only to wonder who brought in the circus.

"He was interesting. But I love fanatics anyway."

Marbury said that for one day of the year, Easter, the Jesus man actually lived the way Christ had. He ate similar food, or what he hoped was similar, dressed like him, and generally spent the day walking around with a cross draped over his shoulders. And everything began at sunrise.

"Why?"

"I guess that's how he celebrated."

I couldn't believe that Marbury was defending a man who was clearly just this short of being institutionalized. But he was.

"Surely you don't buy this, Marbury?"

"Maybe he got people to thinking. You still remember him."

"I remember him because he was so bizarre."

"I'm sure the real Jesus struck some folks as bizarre."

I looked at him but he was smiling.

"Is that what you are, Marbury? A man holding a cross on a street corner?"

"No."

"How do I know that?"

"Well, I could have stayed in Pennsylvania, for one."

Pennsylvania.

That scraping noise was the sound of freedom, said Marbury. Two snowplows fresh off the interstate were already working away on the roads, slowly pushing huge heaps of snow to the rear of the parking lot. Marbury watched them from the window. The sky was clearing by now, a thin ribbon of blue starting to break from the clouds. And sun. Already Marbury could see the dripping of water, melting snow, but there was plenty left. The town had received over three feet of snow, all said, though blowing and other accumulations made that number rise.

It was a ton at any rate.

But the snowplows brought another thing. They brought hope. For the first time since the snow began, things were coming back to normal. Laughter could be heard in the hospital and people whistling. Doctors had a spring to their step. Janitors stole extra-long breaks while the nurses gossiped about everyone else's life.

"What are you going to do once they spring us?"

"Foot massage, if I can find one."

"Not me. A nice, hot shower."

"You can keep your shower, girl. I'm in bed before I shut these eyes."

"I can think of a few other things to do in bed."

Giggle, giggle.

"You girls are crazy. I'm going to treat myself to a good breakfast."

"With real eggs."

"And Belgian waffles with strawberries."

"Strawberries? Where are you going to find fresh strawberries?"

"They'll have to be frozen, I guess."

"I'm eating nothing frozen."

More laughter. Finally one of the nurses asked, "Hey, Father, what are your plans?"

Marbury said that he didn't know. He could continue on to the conference, which was now half over, or he could turn right around and head back to Minneapolis.

"We'll miss you."

And then the nurses went back to their various stations, leaving him alone. He just stood there and watched the snow being moved around. Huge blocks. It was almost over.

The sound of shoes in the hallway. One of the doctors returning. He was wearing a grim expression.

He said, "I'm sorry, Father. The child didn't make it."

Marbury clutched a chair for support. A four-year-old girl. God took a four-year-old girl. That was the only thing he could think of.

"She never regained consciousness. We did all we could but—"

His voice trailed off.

They stood there together and just watched the snowplows. A mound of snow was building in the parking lot the size of a small house. But a house with no windows.

Marbury finally broke the silence. "Have you told the parents yet?"

"No."

"Then let me. I mean I should."

The doctor agreed and shook Marbury's hand good-bye. Marbury said that he walked down to Helen's room preparing in his mind what he would say. But before he could even voice it, say anything, Helen took one look at him and started crying. She already knew that Lucy was dead.

"How did you know?" asked Marbury.

"I had a dream last night. She walked up to me and kissed me and told me that she loved me. I just knew that she was gone."

More tears. Barris held her hand.

"I'm very sorry. Your daughter—"

"You don't have to say it," said Barris.

"She was a special girl."

"I know," said Helen. "She was touched by God himself."

Marbury nodded.

"She lived a good life, Father."

"Four years isn't a very long life."

"We were blessed anyway."

"But she should have lived longer. She might have if not for me."

Marbury felt his head spin, a vertigo of words and sensations.

"I saw the bracelet. She was wearing it and I just assumed that—"

But he couldn't say it. His body started to shake.

Barris touched Marbury on the shoulder, compassionately.

He said, "Don't whip yourself, padre. You couldn't have known."

"Who do I blame then? The nurse, the insulin? What?"

Barris shrugged.

"I should have done something. I was there, Jacob."

"So was God but you ain't hearing nothing from him. My Helen's back and that's the main thing. As for the child, she was always threatening to cure Helen of her diabetes anyway, and I guess she finally got around to doing it."

"You mean—?"

Helen smiled. "Lucy always said that anything was possible with God. Now we know that it's true."

Marbury said that he left as soon as he could after that. Everything else became a blur. He remembered going outside, starting his car, and then driving away but he couldn't say where. And then the police found him walking outside of Altoona.

"You said my car was found in New York?"

"Yes."

"I must have abandoned it. Left the keys inside."

I gave him a look, somewhat incredulous.

"Well, I didn't drive it to New York and walk."

"Maybe you hitchhiked. Anyway, it doesn't matter."

I thought about Marbury's story but I still couldn't figure it out. When I asked him for an explanation he just shrugged.

"I'm just telling you what happened."

"Why did you leave?"

"I told you. What wasn't I responsible for?"

Marbury tortured himself about the bracelet but he had no way of knowing. It probably fell off in the crash and Lucy grabbed it, hoping to return it to her mother. Or maybe that was her intention all along, he said. Make the bracelet vanish and the diabetes along with it.

I said, "You weren't responsible for the snow."

"I drove into it. You said that yourself, Peter."

The snow. Then I thought about the roof. Marbury was up there shoveling but he couldn't finish, which set everything in motion. Or maybe it was already set in motion when he arrived on the scene, I couldn't tell. Water fell onto the generator from the roof, which touched the lives of Helen and Lucy and then back again in a great big circle, all the dots connected, with Marbury in the center.

"Do you believe that Lucy could heal?"

"I do now, yes."

For Marbury said that a strange thing happened to him. He was in the Altoona jail being interviewed for a robbery that he didn't commit but was being accused of when the detective in charge asked whether Marbury wanted coffee. He said that he did. But when the detective reached for the pot it spilled, and piping hot coffee ran down his leg, blistering flesh even through his trousers. The detective was screaming and yelling. Marbury went over and just touched him, nothing odd, for reassurance maybe or just to calm him down, when it happened.

The pain went away.

"I didn't do anything but he thought I did."

"Maybe the burn wasn't that bad."

"Maybe. Except that it happened again."

It was in Minneapolis. Marbury was at the hospital, recuperating after his ordeal in Pennsylvania. He was staying in the neurological ward, a terrible place that was filled with all sorts of cases, from brain disorders on down. Marbury said that he felt stupid being there, especially when there were people worse off than him, but he tried not to think about it, strolling the halls or just watching television. One day he was walking by a room and the door was open. A man was sitting in a bed shaking uncontrollably. No nurses were there. No doctors to check up on him and he was alone.

"I walked in. He didn't say anything. But it broke my heart."

Marbury said that he sat with the man and just held his hand, trying to quiet him down. He prayed too but quietly.

"Nothing left but prayer."

The next day Marbury heard a commotion. People running in the hallway and talking with excited voices. Later he learned that the man, who was suffering from a rare neurological disorder that caused violent tremors in his body, just stood up and walked away. No attribution was made for his recovery, but Marbury said that he knew. It was the spirit of God working through Lucy. Through healers everywhere.

I smiled. "Do you expect me to believe this?"

"Believe what you want."

"I see. And what about your voice? Did Lucy take that as well?"

"I told you already. God decided that I didn't need it."

"You're very cavalier about this, Marbury. Most people would fight to get back what they lost. That's natural."

"Is it?"

"Yes." I was firm.

"Erosion isn't so bad. Dust to dust, just early."

"You can exercise your voice. Maybe surgery."

"The doctors said that I was fine, remember?"

He looked at me, holding my glance.

"Besides, do you really think it would change things if I spoke?"

"It's a start."

"Wheelersburg was a start. And look where it brought me."

I watched Marbury change into his vestments.

People were already filing into the church. I could see them through the window in his office. They were coming up in wheelchairs, some with canes, many of them signing to one another. Whether they were coming for Easter Mass or for a few good words of healing from Marbury, I couldn't tell. But I expected the worst. Cameras, tape recorders and videotape, just to start. I also expected a huge crowd, but I was surprised when I took my seat. The church was barely half full and those that were in attendance didn't seem at all interested in preserving the moment. I saw no cameras. No notebooks. Hardly even a program cracked open.

I also saw the same woman who brought in the baby a few days ago, sitting in front of me. The baby wasn't crying anymore and looked content, all dressed in pink. I tried to crane my neck to get a better view when somebody dropped a hymnal on the floor. Nobody in the place turned their head except for the baby, who wasn't deaf at all but perfectly normal.

God's will, like Marbury said. Except that I didn't know whose will it was. The power of God or the power of Marbury to suggest that something actually happened. I had no other proof than what I saw. A distraught woman, a kiss on the forehead, and now nothing.

My usual problem. Left with nothing.

Someone tapped me on the shoulder.

"Father, I thought you didn't heal?"

It was the woman from the boardinghouse. The one with the arthritis.

"—or are you waiting to be healed yourself?"

"Neither," I said, disappointing both her and me.

"Then let's hope you're in the wrong place."

After she sat down, several rows in front of me, the Mass began. A layperson repeated with words everything that Marbury signed. And I found myself watching and listening to both, like someone in a foreign country with the command of two languages, except the two overlapped in my brain. Each one wrestled for domination. I tried closing my eyes, just to focus on what was being spoken, but I couldn't. Sign language filled my head. I tried to block it out, just hang on every word. I listened to each syllable, every intonation from the lips of the speaker. But still more signs. It had a confusing, almost narcotic effect. Words and signs, fingers darting around verbs and nouns and slipping back into silence again. And the more I watched and listened, the more that I wanted it to end. I wanted it to stop.

It went on this way for almost half an hour before I finally did it. I plugged up my ears with my fingers. No more confusion. I heard the world only one way. The way most of the people sitting there had. Barely a buzz other than the one you imagine to be there and then nothing. Marbury was standing up at the altar alone, praying over the communion elements. The broken bread was raised, then the wine. More prayers. I saw people leave their pews. No rustling from their clothes. No murmuring. No snapping of hymnals. Just silence.

I sat in the far back, observing all of this. I watched people go up and receive communion along with Marbury's prayer. An imaginary cross that he drew on every person's forehead with his finger. Then the words:

Abandon yourself to God.

I was the last in line. Our eyes locked as he handed me the chalice. I drank the wine and felt Marbury's finger on my skin. It was cool. And I felt like I wanted to drift off to sleep.

But I didn't.

Nobody was healed. I didn't see the man who came in on crutches leave in a gallop. The woman with arthritis limped out just as slow as she came in. And the blind woman didn't drop her cane and proclaim her sight. Life wasn't changed at all; it was just the same old life without a disguise.

When I pointed this out to Marbury after Mass, he just shrugged.

"What did you expect?"

I smiled. Maybe I hoped for a miracle.

"People don't always walk away better, you know."

"The deaf girl did."

"She was an exception," he said. "Sometimes no one is healed. Sometimes it takes a week or a month or never. God decides that, not me. And sometimes this is as good as it gets. Blindness, pain, love, too. It's all part of this package called life."

"Why you?"

"Why anything? Why was I at the bar? Why Jill? Why the train?"

The train. Somehow I knew that he would bring it up.

I said, "Believe me, the train wasn't from God."

"I didn't say that it was. Your mother—"

"My mother knew nothing."

"But you were there. You witnessed it."

I was there all right.

"She told me about your testimony, Peter. That horrible man."

"The only horrible man, Marbury, was me."

Sandra was lying on the ground, dead. I just kept staring at her body, which was partially mangled, perhaps too much staring on my part, for one of the train workers laid a coat over her, covering her up. I couldn't believe she was dead. They couldn't believe it either.

"I'm sure I blew the whistle," said one of the men.

Another responded, "We all heard you. It wasn't the whistle."

"Then what?"

Somebody eyed the man from the caboose suspiciously.

"You heard a whistle, right, buddy?"

But the man wasn't listening. He was in his own world.

He said, "Superman tried to fly. He tried but no whoosh."

"What the hell is he talking about?"

"Isn't that the guy who breaks into trains? Sure it is."

"Jesus, you don't think—?"

"He was standing right over her."

❦

"I think he was chasing her."

"Chasing her?"

"I thought I saw him grab her."

"Aw, God!"

The one man grabbed the man from the caboose by the throat. Pressure against his windpipe and gagging.

"You like little girls, Superman? Huh? Do you?"

"Look at him, a fucking pervert."

"Superman tried to fly."

"Christ, his zipper's down. I ought to beat him right here, Jerry."

"What did you do to this little girl?"

"He's a moron. He doesn't get it."

"He gets it. You did something, huh?"

"He did something."

"She was running like hell."

"Running from you, fuckhead."

"Tell me!"

"He killed her."

"I think he pushed her, Jerry."

"Jesus, you crazy bastard."

"I mean his zipper's down."

"Trying to cover it up, he is."

"Well, he's not going to get away with it."

"Let's just beat him now, Jerry."

"Forget the cops. I got justice right here."

And then a fist was waved.

Someone looked at me. "You saw it all, right, kid?"

"He blew the whistle. You heard it, he blew it."

"Just tell me, kid. Did he push her?"

"Don't be afraid."

"He fucking pushed her."

"Did he?"

❧

I don't know how but my head went up and down.

Yes. I answered yes.

That's all the men needed.

"Your next stop, moron, is in hell."

The men were poised to beat him but they didn't. For across the road another group of men from the feed store came running, to see what all the commotion was about. I could see my father running too, limping with that cane of his. But then he saw me, the smoke settling around the train and the other men's expressions, both angry and horrified, and he did something odd. At least I considered it odd. He threw his cane to the side and ran as fast as he could, so fast that I almost thought that he wanted his heart to give out, explode altogether so he wouldn't have to see any of it.

But he did. His daughter was dead.

I shifted my body in the pew, uncomfortably.

Marbury appeared almost stunned, as though he had suddenly been smacked in the face hard. He blinked a few times but he didn't look at me. He couldn't look at me.

"I lied. I told the police that she was pushed. I told everyone that it was the man from the caboose who did it."

Marbury still didn't react.

"My mother didn't even know. I lied to everyone, Marbury."

And the lie had its own power. For the first few days I thought it would blow over and the truth would come out. When it didn't, I told myself that I would tell everyone what really happened but I never did. A week became a month, which turned into a year. Soon all memories were changed. The men from the train believed what they thought they saw, a lie. My parents believed it. As with my brothers and relatives. I found myself exonerated for being there, certainly not to blame for something so hideous, so random. Eventually it became a part of my history, something that if it didn't happen certainly could have.

Marbury looked at me again. He asked me about the man accused.

"What happened to him?"

"He was arrested and taken to a hospital for the criminally insane."

Growing up, I made up all sorts of scenarios for that man. A part of me wanted to believe that he was actually happier there, in the hospital, certainly better taken care of than when he was living in his caboose. I wanted to think that he had more comic books to read, that maybe he was even healed and sent on his merry way with a new life. Then finally I quit thinking about him altogether. He became a shadow memory but a shadow that lurked in the back of my head. And I can still remember his face.

"Why didn't you say something?" asked Marbury.

"I was afraid."

"But you could have freed him."

"Nobody wanted to hear the truth. So I didn't offer it."

And I thought that was true. The police, the men from the train, even my father all wanted an answer right then. They didn't want to hear about a boy not watching his deaf sister around the railroad tracks. They just wanted it neat and tidy. The man from the caboose was perfect. He couldn't fight back; he couldn't defend himself.

"This is a horrible thing to carry with you."

"A lot of people carry secrets. You did."

"Not like this. You should confess."

"I am confessing."

"I mean, to the man himself."

I tried, I told Marbury that. Ten years ago I even went so far as to look up where the man from the caboose had been assigned. I found the facility and actually went there and talked to the superintendent in charge, only to learn that the man had killed himself three years earlier. He had no family. He left nothing. Not even the picture of his mother.

"He vanished the day he met me, Marbury."

"You were goaded into it. I'm sure without the men—"

"The men had nothing to do with it."

"They certainly influenced you."

"I was supposed to be watching her. I didn't. She died."

"People die. People also go on."

It was then that the irony suddenly struck me. I was just like Marbury. Our lives, without us even knowing it, had intersected. But not at this moment. Not even twenty years ago in seminary. They had intersected way before that, when we both were pulled into a place where we didn't expect to be or ever remain.

I said, "Like you I killed a man. Two if you count my sister."

Marbury shook his head. "It wasn't your fault."

"I was in the caboose. Not Sandra. If I hadn't walked in—"

"None of this would have happened."

"Yes."

"I told myself the same thing. But it's worthless, guilt."

Guilt. The worst of sins.

I often wondered how my family would have reacted to the truth. Maybe they would have ostracized me, sent me away and never spoken to me again, or maybe they would have embraced me. Maybe we even would have discussed it instead of erasing the event like so much dust on a chalkboard. But I didn't blame them. What I gave them was a death without any connection. It was just something random, this death, no meaning at all except for the lives it devoured.

"I never told anyone this before, Marbury."

"Why did you tell me?"

I didn't know. A part of me thought that he would understand and maybe that was the reason. Or maybe I had no reason at all.

"At least you came here to tell me, Peter."

"I came here to find out what was happening with you."

"But the reports helped, didn't they?"

I gave him a look and he smiled.

"You know that I wrote them," said Marbury.

"You wrote them? Why would you do that?"

"Call them my bait. You wouldn't have come without persuasion."

I was shocked and angry. Marbury had sent me the reports all along. I began to wonder what was true and what wasn't, whether anything he was saying was true.

And he sensed that.

"Everything I wrote down happened. It all happened," he said.

"What about your voice?"

"Gone."

"You won't even try?"

Marbury just shrugged.

"So you still believe God will help you?"

"I believe you will, Peter."

I was shocked. "Me? You're giving me nothing to work with."

"You've just been given a second chance."

"What are you talking about?"

"I saw you plugging your ears in church."

I was trying to imagine what it was like to be deaf, he knew that. My world had been so closely aligned with silence all my life, except that I didn't recognize it. Silence with Sandra. Silence with the lie that I told. Silence with the peace that I wanted to make with my family. Everything revolved around it.

"You're already halfway there," said Marbury.

He reached into his pocket and pulled out a slip of paper. Then he handed it to me, folded.

He said, "Do it to honor your sister. Do it also for yourself."

I read it and shook my head.

"I can't do this, Marbury."

"You can. Trust me."

"Trust you?"

"Then trust God."

"And what about you? What happens next?"

"I'll wander, think. Maybe live on the beach. I like the sea."

"No cavalry?"

"You were the cavalry, Peter. I always thought you knew that."

I looked at Marbury but he just turned away from me. The sunlight beamed in and through the flowers, the soft glow of Easter lilies around the altar. I could see the simplicity of this place, with its pine pews and cross, and I felt, if for only a moment, that this is what that first Easter must have been like. Rare and perfect. Uncomplicated except for that one thought.

The tomb was empty.

I looked at the piece of paper again.

I said, "I'll speak with the Bishop."

"On God's green earth, what about?"

"Your assignment. It's obvious you can't heal. You can't even heal me. Now if only you spoke."

Marbury seemed surprised.

He said, "But you have documents. The tribunal."

I stood up and walked over to the nearest trash can.

"What documents? I don't see anything."

And they went into the trash.

"Besides, we need a good priest here. And you're the best we have."

Marbury just smiled and followed me to the door. I walked out into the streaming sunlight, the world was all lit up. I went down the chipped concrete stairs and waved to Marbury as he waved back. One of thanks and missing, saying, come back, old friend, life is short and the very best is yet to come.

And then I heard it. A voice as clear as a bell.

It was Marbury.

"Thank you, Peter."

And I didn't turn back.

Milwaukee. Our Lady of Blessing, a school for the deaf.

Present day.

A room full of faces. Bodies in chairs. Books open.

I glance at the piece of paper in my hand, which is old and wrinkled, as if it's been fingered a thousand times. Ancient folds.

My voice:

"I'm Father Whitmore, your teacher here. I'm not deaf but I learned sign language because of my sister, who was. She was about your age."

Eyes back down at the paper.

Marbury's handwriting. A name, an address, a new beginning.

Maybe that's healing someone after all.